HIGHLANDER FOUND

A Scottish Time Travel Romance

REBECCA PRESTON

Illustrated by
NATASHA SNOW

Edited by
ELIZABETH A LANCE

Copyright © 2018 Rebecca Preston

All rights reserved.

Cover design by Natasha Snow

Edited by Elizabeth A Lance

Similarities to real people, places or events are purely
coincidental.

No part of this book may be reproduced in any form or by any
electronic or mechanical means, including information storage
and retrieval systems, without written permission from the
author, except for the use of brief quotations in a book review.

CONTENTS

Mailing List v

Chapter 1 1
Chapter 2 13
Chapter 3 21
Chapter 4 29
Chapter 5 35
Chapter 6 47
Chapter 7 55
Chapter 8 65
Chapter 9 69
Chapter 10 77
Chapter 11 83
Chapter 12 89
Chapter 13 99
Chapter 14 109
Chapter 15 121
Chapter 16 131
Chapter 17 141
Chapter 18 151
Chapter 19 169
Chapter 20 179
Chapter 21 189
Chapter 22 199
Chapter 23 211
Chapter 24 221
Chapter 25 229
Chapter 26 239

Chapter 27	251
Chapter 28	261
Chapter 29	271
Chapter 30	281
Chapter 31	291
Chapter 32	299
Chapter 33	307
Chapter 34	313
Chapter 35	321
About Rebecca Preston	333
Also by Rebecca Preston	335

Sign up for Rebecca's VIP reader club and find out about her latest releases! Click here!

CHAPTER 1

At midnight, Audrina James finally laid her head down, gratefully onto her pillow. It had been another grueling day in Trauma One, it was always the worst when the nursing staff and doctors of the trauma ward lost a child. Audrina looked at the ceiling where she had taped pictures of stars, lush green fields, exotic ancient castles and the forests of her ancestral homeland, vowing to herself that she would visit Claran Castle in Scotland someday. Audrina had put the pictures up so that she could clear her mind of the gruesome scenes that she faced in the E.R. day after day, night after night. They'd worked hard to save the boy from the ravages of a car crash, but Donald Nightingale, of sunny northern California, flatlined at eleven-thirty, after half a day's worth of surgeries, blood transfusions and plasma bags. Audrina didn't cry much anymore after working in the trauma center. But there were a few patients who tugged at her heartstrings. Donald would be one of them.

"Look at the pictures. Look at the pictures," Audrina chanted to herself. She used them as a platform to spring her mind into more pleasant thoughts before she drifted off to sleep. Audrina had been fascinated with the stories and lore of her ancestry when her grandfather used to sit her on his knee and recount tales of his youth, roaming the Highlands of Scotland. That was before a potato famine reached his homeland and forced his family to immigrate to the United States. Audrina would spend hours, daydreaming as she roamed the redwoods behind the house, pretending the tall trees were the ancient forests of Scotland. She knew now that Scotland was much greener, and the forests were made of tall oaks, and rowan trees, beech and pine and ash. But she had promised herself she would visit and discover it for herself someday.

That was all a couple of decades ago, when Audrina had been just seven. After high school, she had gone on to nursing school, and now was faced with the ever-increasing violence of the San Francisco Community Hospital that came through the doors. The timing had just never felt right. There was always one more case to oversee, or one more patient to look after and successfully care for until they walked out the door of their own volition, and not in a body bag or stretcher.

Audrina certainly had the money saved for the trip, but she always felt there was something holding her back. Some small fear she had that there was something Grandfather neglected to tell her about the ancient folklore. Audrina never quite made the jump to buy the plane ticket or book the hotels. She'd never really been sure why, but as she laid there, thinking about all of the never did's that young Donald was never going to experience, she thought, *"Why am I holding back? I have no solid reason, no proof that there is anything in Scotland I should be afraid of."*

"I'm going to request the time off tomorrow and start booking tickets after my trip to the museum," she vowed out loud.

There was no one to hear her proclamation, she realized. There wasn't anyone in her life that she could tell really. *"I guess that makes it kind of sad, maybe even a little pathetic. Sure, I have my co-workers, but they would all say, "Finally, you are taking a vacation," when I tell them,"* Audrina thought.

Audrina had become a trauma nurse after Mom had suffered the same fate as little Donald. She winced as the memories of that day entered her mind. It had been much like Donald's parents rushing into the hospital. The only the difference between her grandfather being informed, and Mrs. Nightingale's heart-wrenching screams, had been significantly different, but as equally as devastating. That's when Grandfather had taken her in. She didn't know who her dad was, and it never occurred to her to go looking for him. She knew that she was loved when Grandfather took her, a scared little girl, home that night. He had cared for her and she didn't need anyone else. Anyone, that was, except her mom, but she wasn't coming back. When Grandfather had passed away when she was twenty-one, she was left with no one. She hadn't even bothered getting a pet. Audrina was never home because she worked so much. She'd always felt like it was her duty to save people because, well, she couldn't save her mom back then.

Audrina tried to roll over onto her side. She was disgusted with herself that she was caught up in her own head and wallowing in self-pity. Her vow was just that and she was sticking to it. She realized, as she flipped back onto her back, that she had never been able to fall asleep unless she was looking up at her pictures. Grandfather had printed them for her the week that Mom had passed. He wanted her to have something to think about, other than the sadness of losing her mom.

As Audrina's eyes began to flutter closed, and she emptied her mind save for thoughts of faraway lands and lost familial ties, something, perhaps the moonlight, sparkled in the pictures above her. A small light that glowed in the tower of the castle, appeared to be brighter in the picture. But she squinted at it, and then chalked it up to fatigue and weary eyes. Her lashes batted against her cheeks one last time, and she fell into a deep, sound sleep.

☙❧

CANDLES SURROUNDED HER IN A CIRCLE, haloing the circular room with an ethereal glow. Long thin tapers of white sheep's fat burned low and lit the gloom of the dark tower. She'd been locked in there for so long, she had lost track of time.

There was a straw mattress, in a splin-

tered bed of Ashwood. The thin blanket cast across it, was worn and frayed at the edges. A small wooden chair, equally as uncomfortable, sat at the base of the bed. It wobbled on three legs, having relinquished one of the legs long ago, for the usage of a handle for a torch. The torch, had long ago burnt to ash, and was scattered and lost amongst the dust and dirt that caked the cold stone floor. She rocked back on her heels and murmured a soft prayer to the Gods, the Spirits, anyone who would listen. The tower was a prison, a tortuous place that seeped into the soul like the smoky blackness of a demon, coming from the bowels of hell to inhabit and ingest the goodness of the person's humanity.

There were bones in the ashes and they cried out to her. Begging her to release them of their captivity. She couldn't help them that night. They would remain tethered there until the angels came for them on the day of reckoning. Thunder clapped outside the castle and lit up the tiny room in an intense light that threw the stark furnishings of the room into harsh contrast. The candles flickered, and she feared they would blow out. Cotswold Castle had many frivolities, protection from the elements in the prison tower, was not one of them.

Rain lashed against the stone tower and sprayed into the room in droves of unending dampness. It rained often in Scotland. She hadn't been dry since she was thrown into that room. The water collected in puddles at the base of the windows. She sat in the middle of the room in an attempt to keep herself and her activities dry.

She knelt over a carnelian kilt pin. It glowed in the candlelight like fire. She reached out her hand and touched it as she murmured. The contact sent a spiral of heat through her fingertips, and she jerked her hand back. How could the stone set in silver be warm to the touch? There was no fire there. The brooch had not been warmed against constant contact with her skin, as she had been shivering since she arrived there. The cold was such that it seeped not only into her bones, but into her very soul. There was no possible way the stone could be warm.

Her eyes fixated on the glowing center of

the gem as she continued to murmur, "Bone of my bone, flesh of my flesh, through spans of time, I cannot rest. Seek thee my kin, and pardon my sin, that I may reincarnate, and new life begin. And with this pin I shall be returned to my love, cast through the ages, by touch of mine blood, and light from sun up above."

The kilt pin glowed ever-brighter in a hue of burnt orange that lit up not only the room, but blazed like the dawning of the early morning's sun, sending spirals of light from the tower window. She heard shouts from below and quickly loosened the stone nearest the door, about halfway up the wall. She hid the pin behind the stone, where someone had hollowed out the stone behind that, and replace the stone so that it looked seamless. She prayed that someone would find it someday, and that she might rise up, released from the ashes of the debris of bodies from that hellish place. She heard footsteps on the stairs and boots clunked up the stone steps. She hurriedly pushed the stone back in place and managed to take one step back, as the door was thrown open and she screamed in terror as…"

☙❧

AUDRINA WOKE, SITTING BOLT UPRIGHT IN BED.

"What the hell?" she muttered as she glanced up at the pictures. *"What the heck was that?"* she wondered to herself as she let her tired body fall back against the pillows. She stared at her pictures and then pushed herself back up to a sitting position. She used her hands and pushed up to stand up, so that her upturned face was almost nose to nose with the picture of the castle. Audrina stared at the tiny light in the tower. It had faded over the years, but she could have sworn last night it glowed brightly. So brightly it almost lit up the room.

And then…and then, that dream. What a strange dream. Who was that woman in the dream? What happened to her? She must have died there. Audrina could feel the drive of her trauma nurse training kick in. She had to save her. *But how? That's silly. The woman…me…that was centuries ago when she cast the spell. And what kind of a spell was that anyway?* Audrina's mind began to fog over, the dream becoming misty around the edges, as reality and the present day slowly seeped back into her mind. She looked around the modern-day bedroom and laughed at the absurdity of her mind's vehemence that the dream was somehow a reality way back when.

She climbed off the bed and hit the shower, enjoying the feel of the warm jets hitting her body as the ache from the previous day's strenuous shift was washed away. She combed out her dark red hair and swiftly braided it down her back as she stared into her own brown eyes in the reflection of the foggy mirror. She wiped away the condensation and flashes entered her mind. The reflection of a woman in the puddles on the floor as the lightening lit up the room. *Did she have brown eyes like my own?* Audrina wondered. She shrugged and finished her braid and then donned her typical casual wear of jeans, an oversized tee-shirt and a ball cap. The ensemble fit well on her athletic frame, and it was just what she needed to walk down to San Francisco's Museum of Natural History.

Audrina enjoyed the casual wear on a rare day off, and she was equally as pleased that the museum was hosting an exhibit on loan from Scotland. She figured she could kill two birds with one stone. She could get her walk in and surround herself in ancient artifacts that made her yearn for a time and place that she had not yet discovered. She pulled her ballcap low over my eyes as she walked out the front door, not minding in the least that she had been accused on more than one occasion of being a tomboy.

CHAPTER 2

When Audrina reached the museum, she purchased her ticket and queued to get in line to be let into the exhibits. She was about ten minutes early and so she began to read the pamphlet that was handed out at the ticket booth. She had been to the museum so many times, she was only interested in the exhibit on loan from the Scottish Museum of Ancient History, but she figured she might peruse a few more on her way out. She read about the various artifacts that were on display, quite impressed with the vast array of items that have been amassed.

As she flipped the cover open, she paused, staring down at the pamphlet stupidly and didn't really register what she was seeing and reading on the pamphlet. As she stared down at the glossy photo, the memory of the dream from last night was a bit hazy, but there was no mistaking the kilt pin from the dream. The one that the woman, that she, had cursed. Or maybe the woman in the dream, she, had placed a spell on it. But there it was, shining back up at her from the brochure. Audrina blinked rapidly in the sun, thinking that maybe she was mistaken, and this was another pin that was excavated from some site in Scotland, and it just looked similar. But as she continued to read, the weighted feeling in her stomach became heavier and heavier.

> *"The Cotswold Pin, a rare and expensive carnelian-gem set pin, was discovered last year in the ruins of Cotswold Castle's eastern most tower. Archeologists and Historians know very little about the pin, except that it was discovered hidden behind a lose stone near the doorway to the tower, where a mason was reinforcing the towers infrastructure. Cotswold Castle is host of a long and bloody history in the Scottish culture and it is well known that Lord Cotswold, imprisoned many native Scotsmen, in his long and cruel English reign over the Scottish people. It is speculated that the pin was hidden by one of*

the prisoners. Most likely in the event of their impending death and the desire for such a rare gem to not fall into the hands of the English. It is known that Lord Cotswold's reign was filled with such terrors and atrocities against the Scottish people, such as imprisonment, torture, and rape. He often invoked the First Rights, also known as Prima, against many young Scottish Brides. It was well known that many of the ones he impregnated he had accused of, tried, and found guilty of witchcraft and subsequently sentenced to death. It is no wonder that whoever was bequeathed such a rare treasure as this gem-inlayed kilt pin, would have wanted it hidden from such an atrocious and vindictive lord and ruler."

Audrina's hands trembled, and the pamphlet shook as she read and re-read the description under the brooch. *"How can this possibly be? How is it that I dreamt of this very kilt pin, only last night? I have no memory of such a pin, even from the countless hours spent with Grandfather pouring over history and ancestry books,"* she wondered.

She only realized that the line had started to move, and people were entering the museum, when someone shouted, "Are you going to stand there all day?"

She jumped and shouted, "Sorry!" over her shoulder as she hastened to the door.

She followed the map of the museum to the new acquisitions and the new exhibit that was on display and it took her a full ten minutes to push through the throngs of people who were gathered around the ancient claymores and thread-bare tartans. She looked for a case, a glass case, figuring, if the museum was going to display rare and beautiful jewelry and gems, they would have it resting on a bed of velvet and enclosed in a high-security, alarm activated case such as the ones she had seen countless other relics, and objet d'art displayed in before.

She found the very case she was looking for and made a beeline for it. She waited at the back of the line and tapped her foot restlessly, as she waited for the older couple who were fawning over the brooches and tartans and listing off their family tree and origins, dating themselves back to the days of yore and their own ancestors. Just when her patience couldn't possibly take any more waiting, the line moved ahead, and she was able to press in, face to face with the kilt pin.

Audrina found it extraordinary that, even after centuries sitting behind a stone, even though it was unexposed to the elements, it was still in pristine condition, as if it had never survived centuries of time passing by. She was sure that it was probably dusty when the mason found it, possibly even the gem was scratched or worn and thus had to be restored, but the pin was pristine.

The brunt orange gem sat at the apex of a silver hill. The silver had been bent and molded onto a swirling pattern to resemble the crest of the hill, so the gem was the representation of the sun. From what Audrina knew of Celtic mythology, the sun symbol was more widely used in the sun cross symbols, which were indicative of Christianity's introduction to the Celtic peoples. But this sun was a literal representation of the sun, suggesting that whoever designed and forged the pin, was still a practicing pagan, possibly giving the pin druidic or witchcraft origins. On the outset of the circular pin, the silver swirled into a Celtic knot which was wavy around the edges, like a river. Audrina knew this because as Grandfather and she had investigated the Claran, or MacClaran name, it was discovered that the Claran's were one of the older tribes of Scotland, but those particular tribes were ancient, nomadic druids who traveled the waters from the Isle of Eire, also known as Ireland. The modern day Claran's were to be found inhabiting the areas on the River Clare and the name Claran literally meant, "One who lives near the River Clare." So, Audrina knew her ancestors had been an ancient people of magics and mystery, and the warring tribes had caused them to take root in Scotland as one of the founding tribes, and they had taken their name and origins with them. The evidence was right there in the pin that resembled the pagan magics and the river beds from whence her people came. The tribes, like the rivers on the pin, were split between Ireland and Scotland.

Audrina felt her excitement at having found such a connection to her ancestors, begin to grow. She stared with her face almost pressed to the glass, willing the pin to do something, anything to give her a sign that she belonged there, with it. She felt like, somewhere deep in her soul, that the pin belonged to her, but she knew this was silly, because it belonged to the museum in Scotland. It didn't change the connection she imagined she could feel through the glass.

As she stood there, she again realized the grumblings of the crowd around her as she had allowed herself to be lost in her thoughts. She was about to exit the line and circle back around, when the crowd was jostled and parted by the streak of a black clothed and masked figure, who shoved them aside. When the intruder got to Audrina, he shoved her so hard, she knocked into the glass and it smashed as the sirens from the museum began to wail. Audrina cut the back of her hand on the glass as she tried to stop her fall, but with the rest of the crowd, she tumbled to the floor. Audrina looked up, just in time to see the masked figure reach into the case and grab something. A flash of orange and silver registered in her mind, and she clawed her way back up and ran after the thief, as he dashed outside the museum with what she could only proclaim as "her" kilt pin.

Audrina chased after him as the wail of sirens from the museum's security, and the automatically notified police screeched in her ear. As athletic as she was, it didn't take her long to catch up to the thief, and she tackled him, expertly maneuvering him into a judo hold from her years of training with Mr. Tanaka at his Japanese dojo. Audrina had needed an outlet for her rage and frustration for losing everyone she had ever loved. And she had miraculously stumbled upon it in the classes offered at the dojo and Mr. Tanaka's ever-patient and serene temperament.

The thief was quickly apprehended at Audrina's capable hands, just as the police showed up and began to cross the sunny court-yard.

"Hey lady, are you nuts?" one of the officer called. "You don't chase after a criminal! What were you thinking!" he shouted.

Audrina didn't answer him, but reached out her shaking hand toward the pin that had fallen to the ground in the take-down of the thief, and as her bloodied fingers from the cut on the glass closed around the pin, the sun shone brightly through a cloud cover, landing directly on the pin, the blood and her hand, and then suddenly, there was a black and gray mist, and Audrina was falling, falling, falling.

CHAPTER 3

Audrina felt something soft and velvety nuzzling her ear. She opened her eyes and wondered why she was being eaten by a great big…

"Is that a cow?" she wondered. She laid on the prickly grass and wondered where the stone courtyard had gone. She remembered looking up into the brilliant sun and she had reached for something, and then, everything had gone black and gray. Audrina pushed up, causing the beast with shaggy brown fur to take a step to the side and she quickly jumped to her feet, clutching her head because it was still spinning.

The cow ambled off down the field a few paces and for the briefest moment, Audrina considered calling it back because at least the cow had been comforting in a weird way. Audrina looked around, confused.

"Where am I?" she asked out loud.

No one answered her, but the cow looked at her with big brown eyes and mooed, happily, and swished its tail.

"It's nice to meet you too," she muttered.

Audrina looked around and discovered she was standing on the offset of some trees. The forest she was standing near was the border line for the field she was in, and at the far edge of the field, she noticed was a farm. She couldn't figure out how she got here because she had just been…

Audrina realized she couldn't remember clearly what she had been doing. She remembered that there was a gray and black mist, and she wondered if maybe she was dreaming. She looked around her and saw something shiny in the grass where she had fallen. She bent over and picked it up. It was an orange and silver pin with a rather peculiar design, but she couldn't remember how she came to have such a pin. Audrina blinked and shaded her eyes to the sun, looking around some more. She found a red ball cap that she picked up and she recognized it as her own. She stuffed the kilt pin in her pocket and donned the ball cap and looked out over the field once more.

At the far end of the field, Audrina saw what looked like a large stone castle.

"Well that can't be right," she muttered. Audrina looked at the cow for support, but the beast snorted at her and continued walking toward the farm. Audrina figured, she might as well see if anyone was home at the farm, because maybe they could help her, so she kept a safe distance as she walked toward the farm with the cow. Audrina had never really interacted with live stock before, having grown up around or in the city of San Francisco.

"That's right. San Francisco," she thought. She had been in San Francisco when she had fallen. Or maybe she had been hit over the head? Audrina stuffed her hand in the pocket of her jeans and her fingers closed around the pin. Flashes of a hooded man jolted through her memory. There was the pin, and then, and then…

It aggravated Audrina to be so confused. She remembered she had been on her way to the museum to see something. She remembered the strange dream she had the night before. She remembered thinking she was going to finally book that trip to Scotland. So why couldn't she remember what had happened at the museum? Maybe she really had waited too long, and now she was cracking up. Maybe this wasn't a dream at all, and she was actually in an asylum somewhere, doped up on drugs that were making her think about all of the pretty places in the world, and not all of the horrible things that happened in the trauma unit. Audrina shook her head, certain that she wasn't crazy.

Audrina continued to walk through the field after the cow, thinking there must be some reason she was in the field. It wasn't like her to visit farm-lands, and as she looked around she also wondered where all the farm machinery was. It seemed rather odd to her that there were no tractors or farm hands or even fences for that matter.

The closer Audrina got to the farm and the stone fortress a few miles beyond that, the more confused she got. Why was there a stone castle in San Francisco? When did they build that? She must be dreaming again, she decided. She often dreamt of far off places when she drifted off to sleep after having stared at her pictures. Audrina began to wonder at what point she had gone home from the museum to take a nap though and that's when she saw a figure emerge from the woods to her left.

Audrina's frown increased, when she noticed the man was wearing a dirty, ragged kilt, over a set of trousers that looked like animal skins. The man who approached her was carrying a crudely made pitch fork of some kind and when he walked up to her, he tossed the pitch fork to the ground near the cow. Audrina gagged at the stench coming from the man and she almost got sick when he opened his mouth to speak to her, and she realized all of his teeth were weathered down to blackened and brown stumps.

She couldn't understand a word he said, but it sounded something like, "What the bloody hell are ye doin', ye wee trollop? Scamperin' round me coos en' showin off yer legs like a common whore in them trews? Aye, well I've got the time this day, ye wee whore, and ye can have a go at me cock with yer pretty mouth first and then we'll spread yer wee legs and have a go at yer fine silky pelt, aye?"

Before Audrina could react or ask him what he was talking about, the farmer lunged at her and tackled her to the ground. He was reaching between his legs and unfastening his pants, and all Audrina could do was try to scream.

He clapped a dirty, smelly hand over her mouth as he hollered, "Haud yer wheest, woman!" while he tried to unfasten the button on Audrina's jeans.

He slapped her hard, and she saw stars in her eyes. She had to shake her head a few times before she could focus on fighting him off again.

Audrina struggled under him, gagging at the stench of his unwashed body as he lowered his head and licked up the side of her neck with putrid breath.

"Stop, stop it! Please!" she cried as his hand found one of her breasts through her tee-shirt and he squeezed roughly. The pain brought tears to her eyes.

The man thrust his hips against hers and she could feel that he was hard and ready, and that she knew if she didn't stop him, he was going to rape her right in the middle of the field.

Audrina reached up and scratched at his grizzled face just as he was about to push her jeans down. She clawed at him while she choked for air, because he used one hand to pin her to the ground, and the other to claw at her jeans.

She managed to scratch him hard enough that she drew blood down his cheek. His misty gray eyes watered and he shouted at her again.

"Bloody bitch!" he roared and slapped her again. This caused her ball cap to fall off and the man froze when her red hair tumbled out from under it and splayed out under her in a fan. The farmer froze on top of her, looking wide-eyed and alarmed.

"It can't be," he whispered.

Audrina struggled under him. She tried to put her clothes back on right. He had ripped her tee-shirt so that her black bra was showing, and she held the two halves of the rip so that she could cover up.

"Maeve? Maeve MacClaran? But yer dead."

Audrina wasted no time at his hesitation. She didn't know who Maeve MacClaran was, but she brought her knee up, catching the farmer right in the groin so that he doubled over and lay on the ground. He was howling with pain when Audrina took the chance and punched him, which caused blood to spurt from his nose. He wheezed as he tried to catch his breath and he rocked back and forth on the ground in pain.

Audrina scrambled up and kicked him one last time for emphasis, so that it ensured she had plenty of time to run and escape the farmer. She shuddered in revulsion as she took one last look at the farmer and then she sprinted toward the farm. She looked back only once to see the cow that had awoken her, was standing over the farmer, and two more, long, shaggy haired cows had joined it. She heard the farmer's curses at the cows, even though she couldn't understand what he had been saying. Audrina didn't waste any more time, she ran to the farm and locked herself inside in order to escape her assailant.

CHAPTER 4

Audrina looked around the tiny farm. There were stalls to the left side that were matted with hay and a few watering and grain troughs and there were storage barrels to the right. She noticed a line of clothing hanging over the back wall directly in front of her and she ran up to it, snatching some of the strange looking pants she had seen the farmer wearing. There was also a white linen shirt and another kilt, but Audrina figured she could dress like a man and go unnoticed even if she didn't have a kilt on.

Audrina bit back her panic. It had occurred to her as she looked down her body as she hastily began stripping, that the attack in the field, wasn't a dream. She came to this conclusion because she saw the bruises that had begun to appear on her skin and she felt the pain in her neck where the farmer had choked her.

Audrina tried to concentrate on anything else. She didn't want to think about the fact that someone had just tried to rape her. She also was in shock that if this wasn't a dream, then the big stone castle she had seen before she was attacked, was also real.

After Audrina dressed and stashed her jeans, ballcap and ripped tee-shirt in an empty sack that she had found hanging on the wall, she looked around and found a large crudely tanned leather, wide-brimmed hat hanging on the wall. She replaced her ball cap for the farmer's hat and tucked her long red hair, up under the hat.

Audrina then looked around at the barrels and she tried to peek in the first one she came across. She couldn't pry the lid off, so she moved onto the next one. Audrina discovered most of the barrels had grain in them, and she couldn't pry open the ones that had seals on them.

When she was done exploring the barn for any useful materials, Audrina carefully unlocked the door and peeked outside. She saw that the farmer was still lying in the field at some distance and she heard his bellows at the cows and could only assume that he was shouting for them to leave him alone. Audrina smiled to herself as she slipped out of the barn and snuck toward the house. Now he knew what it felt like to be accosted and not be left alone or have something that was attacking him not stop when he commanded them too.

Audrina slipped along the wall of the barn, trying not to be noticed. She wasn't sure who else would be around and she felt her heart thumping with anxiety, as she listened at the back door of the small farmhouse.

After a few moments, Audrina took a deep breath, and opened the back door which creaked on its wooden hinges. She blew out her breath and stepped inside the small, one room, farmhouse and began searching the roughly hewn cabinets and drawers that were sitting around the edges of the small house.

The house, or hut, was so small, that only a bed that smelled suspiciously like the farmer was lying in the corner. She had just enough room to stand in the middle of the hut and slowly turn in a circle. Audrina shuddered when she looked at the bed a moment, and she was certain the straw that was the material that made up the mattress, began to crawl. She moved on and saw the table that was sitting in the opposite corner. It was simply constructed, with four legs that sat on top of a piece of wood that had been hastily split. The farmer hadn't even bothered to sand it down and make it smooth. The two chairs that sat around the table were just stumps from a tree that he had cut down and brought in. In the corner by the door, Audrina found two more barrels that were open and inside she found sacks and packages of food in his larder. She helped herself to some of the packages that felt like bread of some kind, and she opted to leave the bloodied packages in the other barrel that smelt and looked like rancid meat.

Audrina filled her sack with as much as she could carry, and she carefully crept out the back door again. She didn't see the farmer in the field anymore, so she decided her best course of action was to walk toward the castle that she saw in the distance. She was sure she could find someone who would help her and wouldn't accost her.

As Audrina walked into town, a plan began to form in her mind. She knew she had to gather information. Based on the bruises she had received at the hands of the farmer and the attack, there was just too much that had happened in the last hour that she could deny that something very strange had happened. That, coupled with the fact that she was walking toward a large stone castle with a bustling, medieval town surrounding it, based on what she saw the closer she got, Audrina knew she was in serious trouble if she didn't gather as much information as she possibly could. She made a silent vow to herself to remain as unnoticed as possible, because if her suspicions were correct, she would be accused of being a witch if she divulged that she believed she had fallen back in time.

CHAPTER 5

As Audrina walked closer to the town, she saw that the buildings in the town that sat at the base of the stone keep, were all made of wood and clay. Some of them were constructed of stone, but she was certain that all of them were from a time period, she wasn't familiar with. The buildings all had large stone chimneys and almost all of them were emitting plumes of smoke, despite the warm summer sun that had been basking down on her for the hour or so that it had taken her to walk to the town. Her eyesight had deceived her, and she had assumed that the fortress had been much farther away than she had originally guessed, but Audrina discovered it was only a mile or so to the town. What had taken her so long to walk there, was the fact that there was a complete and utter lack of a modern rode of any kind.

Audrina had found herself on a cow path of sorts. The muddy road had been clod upon by many hooves and Audrina had had to carefully step around all sorts of animal excrement's as she made her way down the path. She had occasionally glanced back to see if the farmer had followed her, but to her relief, he hadn't.

Audrina's mind raced as she wondered where she was. She had guessed at what the farmer had been saying. He had been calling her a whore and that somehow her clothing was the reasoning for his attack. It didn't excuse his actions though. Audrina felt like she was caught somewhere between reality and a dream. She couldn't possibly have traveled through time to another place, could she? As she neared the town, several horse-drawn wagons passed her by on their way out, and she heard more than one person call out a greeting to her, but she hadn't understood them. They were speaking to her in some sort of broken English, and she felt like it was somehow familiar, but she couldn't quite put her finger on it.

Audrina kept to the sides of the muddy roads that had been so used, they had grooves in the center where the wheels had traveled. The problem she faced as she kept to the sides was that, this was where all manner of refuse had been thrown as well, and it had splashed up like hedges of decayed garbage and waste, human and animal. Audrina had to hold the farmer's shirt to her nose in order not to pass out, and she made her way further into town.

People had begun to stare at her in curiosity, and she hoped the wide-brimmed hat was still hiding her hair. For whatever reason, the farmer had hesitated and been shocked by the sight of her hair, and she felt that somehow, it was something that would stand out to people around here. Most of the people were aged-looking, and there were only a few lanky children who were running around, barefoot in the streets. Audrina began to wonder where all the people her age might be, and that's when she had the uncomfortable realization that, she was looking at them. Their aged and weathered faces were from days spent under the hot summer sun, toiling away at the daily grind of living and chores, all done just so that they could survive. And the winters would be spent nearly half starved once the food stores ran out. Audrina had to shake her head again before she got lost in the idea that she was crazy. She knew she wasn't, but that town and those people were almost too much to process. She needed to gain information and find out not only *where* she was, but *when* she was.

Audrina spotted a marketplace about halfway down the street. She made her way toward it and wondered what she could possibly have that she could trade to add to her bag of food, because she certainly didn't have any money. Then she thought maybe she could get close enough to some people so that she could listen in and start to learn their ways.

Audrina walked between an open fire pit, where a man in a kilt and pants, similar to the ones she was wearing, was roasting a pig over the fire on a spit and selling the bits of meat from the pig to passersby.

"Hock o' ham laddie, for a coin?" the pig roaster called to her. She shook her head and kept walking. She neared a grain stand where a couple of men who were just as rank as the farmer were standing around, haggling over the price of the grain.

"Och, ye shriveled bawbag! Ye cannae ask a coin for ha' a bag o' grain! Tis thievin'!"

"Haud yer wheest. I'll no' be havin the likes of ye tellin' me how tae price me grain!"

"I think the Laird Colin MacClaran ought to hear of yer thievin'! This grain won't even give me Agnus enough tae bake into a wee biscuit e'ry week this winter," the shorter of the two men bellowed.

He was the one that Audrina surmised, was trying to purchase the grain. The taller and burlier of the two was the one selling the grain, and from what little Audrina knew of grain, it didn't look all that great.

From what she knew, grain was supposed to be fine and small, the grain he had in his bags was all different sizes, like he had mixed in the year priors with this year to fatten it up a bit. Audrina knew from when her grandfather talked about it, that grain was supposed to retain moisture for a time, making it have the consistent texture, so the older stuff was pretty evident. But what really captured Audrina's attention was the name MacClaran.

Audrina didn't know much about a Colin MacClaran, but she and her grandfather had studied the MacClaran family tree pretty extensively, because she was a direct descendant of one of Maeve MacClaran's sisters, Catriona, who lived on Skye. Very little was known about Maeve

MacClaran, and whenever her name popped up, her grandfather made it a point to change the subject to another of the MacClaran ancestors or Catriona's descendants. Audrina pretended to browse the stand next to her which offered up various vegetables. She strained her ears and listened hard to the bickering men.

"Och, the Laird has his mind in a ri' state eh? All twisted up o'er the death of his wee bonnie wife, Maeve."

"Aye?"

"Aye, t'was no' but a year ago the wee lass was murder't."

"Nay!"

"Aye. So ye best have done wit it and pay up, man, or leave the grain cause the Laird isnae goin' ta waist his time w'the likes of ye!"

The two men started bickering again and Audrina figured it was time to move on. She had lingered over the vegetables long enough, and the pig roaster had started looking at her suspiciously, probably wondering if she had been contemplating on stealing some.

What had Audrina stumbled upon? Clearly, she was in Scotland. And she was standing at the base of Claran Castle from what she could surmise. She wasn't sure of the date though. Grandfather had skimmed over the dates surrounding this time so much, they were all a bit jumbled in her brain.

Audrina stood back and shielded her eyes as she looked up at Claran Castle. Sure enough, it was just like in her pictures above her bed, but somehow it looked newer, standing here at the base of it. All she had to do was walk a few more minutes up the hill and she'd have been at the gates. The metal somehow looked shiny and newly forged, and the gate in her picture had been centuries old and weathered. If only she could have remembered those dates.

Audrina turned away from the castle, confused and scared. How could she possibly have traveled back in time by centuries? There was just no way that could happen. She felt in the pocket of the trousers she had stolen from the farmer and closed her fingers around the pin once more. It seemed to her like it was a source of comfort because it somehow made it all real. She knew she had gone to the museum and read that brochure. And she was positive she had chased after someone who had tried to steal it, and she had knocked him to the ground and taken the pin back from him. Audrina knew that somehow, the pin belonged to her. She just knew it. Whoever the woman was in the dream, she wasn't sure whether it was Maeve, or her direct ancestor, Catriona, but the woman had cast a spell over the pin, and it had found her centuries later and called her home.

Audrina decided to cut down a side street as she let her thoughts wander. She felt sure it was safer this way than being out in the open. She side-stepped a body lying on the muddy ground and her nursing instincts kicked in. She leaned over the body which was lying in a puddle of what smelt like bodily fluids and really strong ale, and she began to reach her fingers toward the direction of what she hoped was the neck to check for a pulse, and then the body jerked and bellowed.

"I'll be havin' another dram!" he shouted and jerked, sending a few coins rolling across the mud-covered stones that were pounded into the road. Audrina grabbed at the coins as she heard the man take a deep breath, and then let out a loud rumbling snore as he went back to sleep in the mud.

Audrina scurried backwards after relieving the man of the coins he had so carelessly lost in his drunken stupor, and she pushed into a door that she felt behind her and stepped into a dimly lit room. There were men surrounding her and she felt her heart beat faster as she sidestepped drunken men lying on the floor, and she skirted around the corner of tables, until she found herself in a corner near an empty table.

Audrina sat down and breathed a sigh of relief as she looked around the small room. It was an ancient pub that hosted bar stools and rough table tops. The mugs that scattered the tables were roughly shaped clay mugs and the men were all wearing kilts and shirts. Some had pants on and others she could see scabby dirty knees poking out from under the kilts.

The only other woman who was in the bar was obviously a bar maiden of some kind, but it was clear the way the men scooped their hands down her low-cut dress, she wasn't a maiden as she didn't even bat an eyelash when they'd give her breast a jiggle and a squeeze. She was plump with wiry blonde hair and yellowed teeth. Her pudgy cheeks were red with exertion as she hefted her ample body around tables and over sleeping drunks.

She sauntered her way over and asked, "What'll ye be havin' laddie?"

Audrina threw a coin down on the table and grunted, "Drink."

The bar maiden looked at her for a long

moment, but then shrugged and slammed a clay mug on the table. She took the flagon she was holding and poured Audrina a drink. Without another word, she turned on her heel and went back to the group of men congregated around the bar.

"As I was sayin', laddies, the Laird himself was in here ha'in' o'dram o'ale and—"

"Bollocks, Maudie!" one of the men shouted at her.

Audrina flinched when Maudie hauled off and slapped him so hard he fell of the bar stool. As the other men laughed, Audrina watched as the man stood back up, laughed himself and climbed back on his bar stool.

"As I was sayin', the Laird himself has been in a ri' state o'mind w'it the death o'his Mauve. A year ago today in the year o'our Lord, 1304. I says the Laird is bidin' his time, waitin' for the Sassenach Bastards tae make a move. Then he'll rip through 'em wit claymore an fire in his soul. Aye, I speak truth, lads. The Laird's out for revenge."

The men nodded and grunted at her as Audrina sipped her ale. It was bitter and vile and so strong it turned her stomach. Audrina realized, 1304, was only ten years before the Scottish uprising in the

Battle of Bannochburn. The Scottish and English were right in the middle of their long and bloody war and Robert the Bruce would claim Scotland a free country in only a decade. But the hostility between Scotland and England was just starting to escalate. Edward the First would reign as King of England for another three years until his death in 1307 and William Wallace would begin his campaign to rouse the clans against the English. Whatever had happened to the Laird Colin's wife Maeve, Audrina was sure it was due to the hostility between the Scots and the English.

Audrina got up and made her way toward the door. She kept her head low and almost made it to the door when she heard one of the men say, "Aye, Cotswold. The bloody Bastard. Done Maeve wrong tae be sure."

Upon hearing the name Cotswold, Audrina clutched her head. The name triggered something in her mind that had her thinking about the dream. Bile rose in the back of her throat. At first, she thought it was the ale, but the more she thought about the name, the more the nausea grew.

"Och, laddie, ye alright?" Maudie called.

Audrina waved her hand at her and lurched out the door.

Once out into the side street, Audrina leaned over and clutched her head. Memories of the night she had been locked in the tower, of when the woman was locked in the tower came slamming back into her. Revulsion, hatred, fear and rage rose up inside her and threatened to consume her. The name Cotswold was a catalyst to the feelings and she wasn't sure she could overcome the overwhelming emotions. Audrina sucked in a few deep breaths and tried to inhale a fresh breath of air, but she couldn't get the stench of the area out of her nostrils. She stumbled toward the entrance to the alley and made her way down the street and toward the forest on the opposite end of the keep. Audrina needed time and space to process. She didn't understand how she and the dream fit into everything that was going on, but she understood the more she immersed herself in the fourteenth century, the harder it was going to be to get home to the twenty-first century.

CHAPTER 6

Audrina decided to hide out in the woods on the far side of the keep. She figured it was the best place to regroup and think about what she was going to do. She had thought about it and came to the conclusion that the kilt pin brought her to that year, it was somehow going to get her back, but she needed to be far enough away from everyone in the town to think clearly and not draw attention to herself.

As Audrina cut through the side streets and ducked behind huts and stores, she picked up stray items she found lying in the mud, and decided she would rely on her nursing training, which not only had included trauma training, but survival training as well. She was going to make a makeshift shelter until she could get back to the same field, without the famer finding her, and try everything she could think of to return home. Audrina found some rope and stray bits of woven cloth from sheep skin. She gathered the items thinking she could make a tent or a hammock of some kind to sleep off the ground, and she used whatever supplies she could stuff into her stolen bag.

Once free of the town, she circled around the keep which was surrounded by a large moat and found herself at the back side of the fortress and standing on the edge of the fen. Audrina decided that she could risk walking along the edge of the fen until she reached the woods, because it was unlikely anyone had been back here in quite some time. The grass had grown up to almost her waist, and there were no discernable walking trails, so she has assumed that everyone stuck to the main part of town and didn't stray too far from the shelter of the keeps stony walls.

As Audrina walked, she let the beauty of the nature seep into her mind, relaxing the whirlwind and emotion that had been building ever since she woke up in the farmer's field. The fen was quiet pretty and the tall grass swayed in the warm summer breeze. Audrina recognized some of the trees from the pictures of her bedroom, and she was comforted by the familiarity of that.

Audrina listened to the bird's chirp and small creatures scurry in and out of their hidey holes and she paused once when a great rustling sound came from her right. She wasn't prepared to deal with any large predators, although she highly doubted a bear would roam this close to the castle, but it was always possible a mountain lion had come down from the hills. Audrina froze, as the head and antlers of a great red deer, rose up from the grass a few feet away where it had been munching. She stood stock still as she and the deer regarded one another, and then she jumped a little when the deer took off in the opposite direction. It ran for cover amongst the trees at the far side of the fen and cleared a considerably wide path for Audrina to follow in its wake.

Once Audrina made it halfway through the fen, she had to jump over a small stream and she began stepping carefully as the ground had become wetter and soggier. She stopped, wondering if she should try to travel in the trees for the rest of the way, she was afraid she was heading into a bog of some kind. Scotland had always been known for its surprising terrains and with all the documentaries she had watched with her grandfather, she knew with any wrong mis-step she could end up waist deep in muck and mire if the grassy cover gave out under her feet.

Audrina looked at the thick cover of the trees and they looked dark and foreboding. She decided to continue chancing her luck with the field because she didn't know anything about what might be lying in wait amongst the trees, and she had already had enough surprises, toils and struggles for one day.

Yeah, because time traveling for seven centuries certainly could fall under all three of those categories, she thought to herself.

Then she snorted out loud at the ridiculousness of the thought and caused a flock of geese to rise up a few feet from her left and fly away. It startled her, and she clutched a hand over her chest as she regained her composure. She wasn't sure how much more she could take, until she heard the sound of someone crying for help.

She wasn't sure she heard it the first time, so she paused and waited, and then sure enough she heard a muffled, "Help!"

Audrina hesitated, unsure if she should believe what she had heard. After all she had been through that day, she had been beginning to wonder if she could even trust her own mind. Then she heard it again.

"Help! Please! Help!"

Her instinct took over. She had heard those words hundreds of times in her nursing days. Families of loved ones who brought their loved one into the E.R. and cried, "Help, he's bleeding!" or "Help! My toddler stuck her hand in the bleach bucket and sucked on her fingers!" Audrina began to run toward the cries. The closer and closer she got, the louder they became and the more frantic they became.

She looked around, trying to find the source of the cries, but they had gone silent for a moment. She began frantically searching through the grass, hoping whoever was in danger would cry out again, and set her back on the right path.

Audrina heard the thumping, and squishing sound of hooves coming toward her in the wet grass, and she froze on the spot as the horse thundered past her. Only once it had cantered past, she had the thought to jump out of the way, but by then, the horse had taken off at a gallop and was all the way across the field near the castle. Audrina thought it was strange that the horse was rider less, especially since it was wearing reins and a small saddle.

Audrina heard the cry again to her left. Audrina wondered if the person who was calling for help had fallen from their horse and they were injured.

"Help!" It sounded garbled, like whoever was in trouble couldn't catch their breath. Audrina raced toward the sound and pushed her way through a cloak of overhanging vines and tree branches, so that she was standing on the edge of a bog. She looked around and found there was a boy in the middle of the bog. It appeared as if he had tried to cross the bog on his horse on an old mossy log, and the log had finally decayed enough and split in half, sending the boy tumbling down into the muck and mire. The horse must have reacted on instinct and managed to get out of the bog and run away, but it was clear the boy was not so lucky, having been thrown deeper into the bog.

Audrina sprang into action and searched the edge of the bog for a branch big enough to support the boy's weight so that he could grab on and she could pull him out. When she spotted a downed tree halfway around the bog, she raced toward it and tugged at the deadening branches as hard as she could, until one broke free. Audrina dropped her bag and turned back to the bog, dragging the branch behind her. She decided the best way to get to the boy was to climb along the first half of the log he had been on, and then extend the branch so he could grab hold.

She carefully edged her way out onto the log, which began crumbling around her sneakers, and she ended up having to squat down on her hands and knees, because a couple of times, the log disintegrated under her feet and she ended up knee high in the water.

The boy spotted her and flailed his arms in her direction, only further causing himself to sink in the gooey slime.

"Try to stop moving!" she called, but it was no use.

Panic had set in and the boy's fight or flight instinct had kicked in and he continued to thrash around and try to grab onto anything he could reach.

Once Audrina made it to where the log had fallen into the water, she hooked her shoe under a branch on the log and crept out on her hands and knees as close to the water as she could get. She held the branch out to the boy and extended her arm and torso as far as she could so the branch would reach him.

Just as the boy's head fell below the surface of the water, Audrina cried out to him one last time, "Grab on!" and she felt the boy's hand close around the end of the branch.

CHAPTER 7

The boy swiped at the stick a few times and missed, and on the third try, he latched onto the stick. Audrina pulled with all her strength and the boy slowly squelched toward her through the mud. When he was within grabbing distance, Audrina linked her arms under him and around his torso and began pulling him out of the water.

The boy was young, less than ten was Audrina's guess. He started to cry when he began spitting mud and slime as Audrina hugged him closer. Before she could get him back up the log, the combined weight of them caused it to snap, and sent them both crashing back down into the bog.

Audrina reacted quickly as she gagged on the

foul stench of the putrid bog. She grabbed a low overhanging branch and pulled herself and the boy that she had one arm wrapped around, toward the bank and the tree which was rooted just off shore.

As the two collapsed in a muddy heap on the mossy bank of the bog, they were both breathing hard and soaked through from the wet sludge of the bog.

"Are you ok?" Audrina asked the boy, but he was still too panicked to answer her. He clung to her neck in a hold that Audrina knew only too well from the trauma center. He couldn't think rationally and probably wouldn't for quite some time. She rocked him back and forth in her arms as they sat there another few moments.

After a few minutes, Audrina heard shouts in the distance and the boy looked up. He had startling big brown eyes and was just a slip of a boy in her arms. He stood up and began running toward the sounds as men came into the woods.

"Donal! Och, wee laddie! Yer alrigh'!" a man shouted as he scooped him up in a bear hug. "When we saw Fergus come runnin w'it nary a rider...och how many times have I got t'tell ye, nowt t'be ridin the beast out here in the bog!" the man thundered down at the boy.

For a minute, Audrina thought the boy was going to cry again, but he swiped at his face, which only worsened the muddy mask that was already caked on and kicked his chin up.

"I'm no' a wee lad, Colin! I can ride better than all the lads in town!" His bravado only wavered a little as the men around Colin began to chuckle.

Audrina picked her bag up that she had set down, and was hoping to slip away quietly when one of them shouted, "Oye, you there? Where d'ye think yer going?"

Audrina froze and turned back to the group.

"That's the lad tha' saved me, Colin!" Donal told him.

Audrina looked down at herself, remembering that she was covered in mud. Her face must be masked too.

She made her way around the bog to join, them, unable to avoid the confrontation. As she approached, she noticed Colin stood almost a head taller than the rest, but had startling blue eyes that were sunken in a mask of responsibility and a guarded nature.

Audrina looked around at the rest of the men and noticed their large swords they carried on them and decided she didn't think it was a good idea to try to run from these men. She hadn't meant to be noticed, but she stood there waiting for one of them to speak to her.

"Is it true, lad? Ye saved wee Donal here?" the man with the bushy red beard asked.

Audrina nodded, but didn't speak.

"You've just rescued the wee brother to th'clan, Laird boy. What say ye t'that?" he asked again.

Audrina shrugged, not knowing what she should say. She didn't want to give away her disguise since they all still thought she was a boy.

"Come on lads, let's get back t'the castle. Mum's past her wits w'it worry, Donal."

Audrina trudged along behind them as the men gave her slaps of approval on her back which almost sent her sprawling. She didn't want to go with them, she would rather have been left alone, but Donal was weaving a tale of daring escape and rescue in which, he'd barely escaped with his life, and she, known as the lad, to them all, barely made it to him in time and just only managed to help him. The men seemed to know it was a tall tale because the more outlandish Donal's story got, the more they snickered and looked at her.

Colin didn't spare a backwards glance at her as

they walked back through the fen and Audrina was left worrying about how she could slip away.

Shouts and cheers went up as they rounded the moat and stone walls of the castle. The inhabitants all seemed to be hanging on with bated breath to see that Donal was alright.

As they entered the castle, Audrina spared a glance to look around. They were in a long hallway with many tables in rows and then a long table at the head of the hallway near the huge fireplace. Large torches and chandeliers with wax candles in them burned around the room, and several stone alcoves led to doors that Audrina wondered what was behind them.

The men all made their way to the tables to join the crowd, and Colin led Audrina and Donal to the left through a doorway that hid a staircase. As they spiraled up the stairs, Audrina had to pay attention, so she wouldn't trip because they were so steep and narrow, and only lit every few steps by a small glowing torch.

Once they crested the last step, she followed Colin as he led them down a dark hallway, sparsely furnished and through a doorway at the end. They were in a bedroom of some kind and a woman was standing at the window, wringing her hands in her dress. When she turned around, Audrina knew instantly it was Donal's mother, because she let out an anguished cry and raced to him, hugging him to her chest.

"Donal! Och ye've given me a right scare, lad! What were ye thinkin' ridin' out in th'bog like that? Och, ye wee devil, I'll tan yer hid fer this!"

But the woman just hugged Donal closer to her. She had sunken eyes like her eldest, but hers were green and her small thin frame threatened to collapse in on itself. Donal tried to pull away from his mother, but she held fast to him and began thanking Colin.

"T'wasn't I mother," he spoke in a gruff voice.

Audrina felt uncomfortable as both of them turned to her.

"T'was the lad here."

"Och, thank-ye!" his mother exclaimed.

Audrina nodded, still remaining silent.

"What's yer name, laddie?" the woman said softly.

Thinking quickly Audrina said, "Argus." It was her grandfather's name and since he was from Scotland, she was praying it was safe to use. Her voice was gravelly and raw from ingesting so much swamp water and so she prayed they continued believing she was a boy.

"Well. Argus, ye both look a fright. I'll have Mary send something t'eat up and ye'll be havin a bath. Both of ye. Ye smell worse than the stench o'the dogs when they swim in tha' water." The lady crinkled her nose and shushed Donal when he began protesting.

Audrina was glad to see the two of them squawk at each other. In a way, Donal was the Donald Nightingale she didn't get to save. But she somehow felt relieved in her chest that this somehow made up for it a little.

She turned to the door when Colin indicated she should leave. She would be grateful for the food, but she wasn't sure how she was going to escape the bath. If she washed the mud off now, her disguise would be gone, and she didn't want to be caught having to explain. As it was, being around so many people was risky enough.

Colin ushered her into a room that was adjacent to the woman's and found that it was very similar to the one she had just left. There was a bed, a table and chairs, and someone had set out a large tub and filled it with water. A bar of soap and a linen had been set beside the tub, and just as Colin was about to leave, a small woman in a plain linen dress with an apron and cloth hat came in without a word and set a plate of food on the table.

Audrina looked at it longingly and then back at Colin.

"There'll be clothes in t'chest for ye." He indicated to the great wooden chest that sat at the foot of the bed. "Wash up now, I'll expect me mum, will be wanting t'hear yer story. Ye've saved m'youngest brother, Donal. I expect my other brother will be wanting t'hear the tale as well."

He closed the door behind him without another word. Audrina looked around in panic, wondering what she was going to do. She went to the chest and found a clean set of pants and shirt. Her sneakers were completely ruined, but she discovered an old pair of boots under the bed and they were only a size too big, so she sets them aside with the rest of the clothes.

Audrina wanted nothing more than to sink into the water. She dipped her fingers in the water and it was tepid, but not unpleasant. She yearned to scrub away the mud and filth and she would have been grateful to wash away whatever felt like it was crawling through her hair. Unable to ruin her disguise, Audrina turned away from the tub and sat down to eat.

Audrina didn't trust the meat on the plate. So, she ate the fruit and breads that were there instead. She realized she was ravenous and didn't hear when someone came back in the room.

CHAPTER 8

Audrina didn't see the man who was standing in the alcove of the doorway. She continued to pick at her food and eat bits of bread and cheese from the platter.

"I thought ye might like t'dine w'it me and t'family tonight and recount yer tale, lad." The gruff voice of Colin sounded from the alcove.

Audrina jumped and scuttled backward toward the bed and the corner of the small chamber. It was a small room and she hid in the shadows of the one window that let a cool breeze in. It was growing darker outside and the pale light cast a glow around Colin as he stepped into the room.

"Och, lad, come away from the shadows. I'll not hurt ye. Ye saved m'brother. I ken ye might want t'tell the great hall how ye did it. Yer a hero now, lad." Colin stood with his legs slightly apart and his hands on his hips. He was so tall and she observed how he wore his kilt over a pair of pants, just like the farmer had. He had on a clean white shirt where Donal had muddied his previous one. Colin's long silver-blond, unkempt hair and scruffy beard made him look fierce in the low light. It was as if his presence in the room dominated the space, and left Audrina with no way to escape. Audrina didn't say anything, nor did she move away from the shadows of the corner. She really didn't want to go to the great hall and tell anyone anything. She wasn't sure how she was going to get out of this mess.

Colin looked around and saw the bits of food missing from the tray and then he looked at the tub.

"Ye've not taken yer bath. Mum won't allow ye at the table still lookin' like that. Ye'd best wash up, lad."

Audrina hesitated before moving away from the wall. She had one chance and one only to escape the situation. She figured she would surprise the young Laird and pretend she was going to get in the tub, and then dash behind him and out the door before he could catch her. Her plan seemed solid in her mind; that was until she was sure she felt something slither through her hair from the soggy hat and bog water. She screeched and batted at it, sending her hair in a tumble down her back. Colin's hand immediately went to his sword and then he froze as Audrina stepped into the light from the window.

"It cannae be," he whispered.

Audrina pulled the slimy bug from her hair and shuddered as she flung it away from her. She wasn't sure what he was talking about, but she was fairly certain with her screeching her cover had been blown.

"That hair," he whispered and reached a hand toward her.

Audrina didn't know what he was talking about, so when he strode over to her in two great bug steps, she was completely caught off guard and by surprise when he pulled her into his arms and began kissing her.

Audrina had never been kissed by a man quite like that before. His lips and tongue were hot and possessive, and he claimed her mouth with his own. Audrina couldn't help the warm feeling that began to glow in her as it started to ignite her nerve endings in a passionate fire. Colin wrapped his arms around her further, deepening the kiss and tangling his fingers in her hair. For a long while, Audrina got lost in the feel of his tongue darting in and out of her mouth. When Colin deepened the kiss, she willingly succumbed to the onslaught of his mouth, as he growled into her lips and she moaned softly before realization of what she was doing struck her.

CHAPTER 9

Audrina's consciousness seemed to slam back into her and she began to struggle in Colin's arms.

"Let go of me! Stop it!" she cried.

Colin seemed equally as confused as she was when she squirmed and attempted to get away. "It's alright, lass, ye'r home now. We can be at peace w'it one another and put it behind us. Bloody hell, woman, would ye just hold still!" he thundered.

Audrina pushed against his chest and tried to get him to let go. How had she become so caught up in Colin's kiss? Had he kissed her because like the farmer, once he found out she was a woman, he decided it was perfectly ok to accost her? Audrina realized she was blushing furiously when she finally managed to break free of his arms. She hadn't anticipated on enjoying the kiss so much, but no one had ever kissed her with so much passion before.

"Maeve, t'will be alright, lass. Just calm down," Colin encouraged.

"I'm not Maeve!" she insisted.

"Sure ye are, lass. He's gone and broken ye he has. T'as been nigh a year he's kept ye. That's no' the way Prima Noctem is supposed t'be upheld. He was supposed tae return ye the day aft that dreadful nigh. But yer home now, Maeve," he insisted.

Audrina crinkled her brow in confusion. *Why was he calling her Maeve?* She tried to make him see again.

"I'm not Maeve. I woke up in the field. I swear it. My name is Audrina James. I don't know who this Maeve is you are talking about!" She stamped her foot for emphasis.

Colin regarded her like a child and tried to smile at her reassuringly.

"Och, Maeve, I'd recognize that hair o'yers anywhere. Runs red as blood it does."

Audrina folded her arms over her chest and tried to back away from him. Colin kept a firm grip on her elbow and pulled her toward the door. When he got there he opened it and shouted, "Mother! Alasdair! Make haste and come quick!"

Colin pushed Audrina back into the room and stared down at her with a look of pure wonder and love. It made Audrina uncomfortable because she barely knew the man.

Audrina heard the sound of footsteps approaching and the door was flung open again.

"Colin, upon my word, what?" But Colin's mother trailed off when she caught sight of Audrina's hair.

"It cannae be!" she exclaimed.

A man came in after her. He was slightly shorter than Colin, but Audrina recognized him as one of the men by the bog. He wore the same color tartan as Colin and had the same blond hair and blue eyes, but he did appear a year or two younger than Colin.

"Aye, t'is what I said." Colin looked between his mother and brother.

"Maeve?" His mother stepped forward.

Audrina flinched back when she raised a hand as if she was going to touch her hair.

"Maeve, lass, it's me, Mary. I knew yer mam when we were wee babies. T'is a shame ye lost them so early."

Audrina tried to make her understand. "I'm sorry, you've got me confused with someone else. I'm Audrina. Audrina James from San Francisco, California. Please, I know it sounds crazy, but I'm not Maeve. I woke up in a field and then was accosted by this farmer, but I think it has something to do with this pin…" Audrina searched her pockets for the pin, but it was gone. "It was here. I had it, it was here!" she cried.

"Lord, Mercy!" Mary cried. "Colin, look. She's must ha' dropped yer wee bauble on her journey home. But she kept it, she remembered."

"Lass, don't ye remember? I gave it t'ye the nigh' His Lordship took ye. I told ye t'was only one nigh' ye had to endure in the arms o'tha' monster and if ye held this, ye'd know I was wi' ye helping ye endure."

Audrina shook her head giving up on finding the pin. "No, you don't understand. Please listen! I'm not Maeve, I'm an ancestor. I went to the museum, they had a Scottish exhibit and this pin was on display there. Someone tried to steal it and I chased after them. When I knocked him down, that's when I touched the pin and then I was here, in this time, in the field. I swear to you, I'm telling the truth! I walked to town after the farmer tried to rape me and I gathered supplies while I learned I was sent back seven centuries ago and then decided to make a camp until I could figure out what to do."

Colin's brother Alisdair stepped up and looked hard at her. He had a light scar running down his cheek which made Audrina tremble in fear. They had to believe her. If they didn't, what was she going to do?

Finally, he stepped back and smiled at her. Just when she was starting to think someone believed her, he turned to Colin and said, "He's a cruel man, he is. Almost took m'eye the last I was in his clutches. Bloody Bastard!" He pointed to the scar on his face. "T'is no wonder the lass' wits are addled. He had her in his clutches over a year, ha'his way w'it her and dumped the poor lass in a coo field."

Colin nodded his head and looked at Mary. At that moment, Donal came bursting into the room.

"Och, lookie here, laddie, Maeve has been returned to us. She's no' dead after all!" Colin cried.

"No, please. I'm not Maeve! I swear to you." She tried beseeching Mary, but the woman's gaunt face was flush with excitement and her eyes shone with tears.

"Such a sweet lass y'are, no' havin' yer wits but

savin' the wee lad anyway. We always had a laugh we did when he'd be up tae his antics." Mary walked over and patted her on the cheek. "T'will be alrigh', dearie. We'll look after ye o'course."

Mary turned on her heel and began shooing the men from the room. "Go on w'it ye. Give the lass some time tae come t'her senses. She needs a bath she does." She shooed the men out the door and they stared at Audrina as they went. There were mingled looks of excitement, concern and love from Colin. Mary turned back to Audrina and said, "It's been a long hard journey for ye, go on and have a bath, t'will make ye feel better."

She pointed to the tub and Audrina walked over to it slowly. She looked down into the clear water and saw the reflection of her muddy face staring back at her. She realized then, just how thoroughly exhausted she was. Mary went to the trunk and pulled out a simple linen dress and a pair of slippers and laid them out on the bed for Audrina.

"Call me back when ye're ready to wash yer hair and I'll halp ye," she said softly. She walked to the door and closed it behind her, but Audrina heard the loud click of the lock behind her as she found herself locked in the room.

Audrina stripped off her muddy clothes and

placed them in a pile beside the tub and stepped into the water. It was considerably cooler, but in the sticky summer heat, she felt it was refreshing as she grabbed the soap and began to lather it over her skin, as she washed away all the sediment from the bog. Audrina wasn't accustomed to anyone helping her bathe, so rather than calling Mary back into the room, she washed her hair and then wiped up where she had splashed water around the tub with the linen that was left with the soap.

She pulled on the dress which was just about the right size for her and she tried to tie the laces at the back, but was unable to do so herself. Instead she opted to comb her hair with her fingers and was just working through the last of the tangles and snarls in her hair when a soft knock issued at the door.

CHAPTER 10

Mary stepped back through the door and smiled at Audrina. Audrina backed away swiftly, still wary of the woman.

"T"is alright, lass," she said softly to Audrina.

She looked at Audrina's wet hair and then went back to the door, calling someone to come in. The woman who had brought food for Audrina came in with another woman who was clearly a servant of some kind, and together the women lift the tub up and remove it from the room.

"I suspect ye feel a wee bit better then, aye?" Mary asked Audrina.

"Yes, the bath was nice, thank you," Audrina replied. She knew the woman didn't mean her any harm, but she had to make her see somehow.

Before Audrina could think of anything else to say that would convince her, Mary said, "Aye, I suspected ye wouldnae want tae be touched after he got his hands on ye. T'is good ye washed yer hair though, lass. T'was crawling w'it vermin."

Audrina suspected whoever *he* was, wasn't Colin, but she nodded her head politely as she gazed around the room. It brought on a feeling of déjà vu. She felt like she had been there before, but she knew that wasn't possible. Audrina circled the room, touching the stone walls and the small table. She warmed her hands by the crackling fire in the hearth. She looked at the bed and felt like, she knew this place somehow. What she didn't understand was, why had there been men's clothes in the trunk as well as women's? Why did this room seem so fond to her, when she had never set foot in it? She walked over to the nightstand which was only a small wooden table roughly carved and smoothed over. She fingered the lace that was draped over it, having been knitted to fit the table top width. There was a small portrait propped up on the stand. It made her curious so she picked it up.

"I'll lace yer gown for ye lass if ye don't mind?" Mary asked softly from behind her.

She nodded and felt Mary's frail hands at her back, tying the gown up.

She turned her attention back to the small likeness, it was a crude painting of three women, but they all had distinctive features. Audrina recognized one immediately, she had the same flaming red hair as Audrina. This must be Maeve everyone kept telling her about.

"Mary…" she began.

"Aye, lass?" Mary finished with the laces and stepped back.

"Mary, can you please listen to me. Just listen to the whole story and then if you still think I'm Maeve, please…" Audrina implored.

Mary looked at her kindly then sat on the edge of the bed and patted the soft cushion below her. It was a finer mattress than the one she had seen in her dream, but it still crunched under her, indicating it was straw, stitched into the material. But at least it wasn't straight straw.

Audrina sat on the edge of the bed and looked at Mary. She was so tired, and Mary had been so sweet to her, she just wanted someone to listen to her.

"Alright lass, tell me yer story from the top, and

I'll then tell ye about our Maeve. We'll see in the end how they match up, aye?"

Audrina blinked back the tears of gratitude. She was so grateful Mary was finally going to hear her out, and listen. She told her everything. She started with the death of her mother and having to live with her grandfather. She told her about how he raised her in believing in the magic of Scotland, and ever since she was a little girl she had the strongest sense of fernweh, the wanderlust, the yearning to travel to this far off place because somehow it felt like home. She told Mary about when her grandfather died and how she threw herself into her job as a trauma nurse and more than a few times, Mary's brow creased in confusion.

She had to explain what a trauma nurse was to Mary who briefly interrupted to say, "Aye, a healer. I ken what that is."

Audrina continued and told her about little Donald Nightingale and how she had lost him in the trauma unit. She told Mary about going to sleep that night and making the vow that she would visit Scotland finally. She told her about the strange dream and the woman in the dream and the kilt pin. She told her about reading the brochure and seeing the pin on the paper and rushing to see it in the case. She felt breathless as she told her about the thief and how she chased him and knocked him down. Then she recounted how she had been sucked into the gray and black mist and she woke up in the field and was accosted by the farmer. She finished her story with the tale of sojourning into the city to discover where she was, and when she was and how she decided to camp out in the woods and that's when she found Donal.

Mary had grasped her hand halfway through the story, and she didn't mind. It was comforting somehow, and Audrina felt her patting her hand as she finished her tale.

"Och, lass," Mary whispered with tears streaming down her gaunt face.

"Do you believe me?" Audrina whispered hopefully.

"I believe…" she began as she gazed into Audrina's hopeful face. "I believe ye think t'is real."

Audrina's face fell as she realized Mary didn't believe her. She started to say something, but Mary held up her other hand.

"Nay, lass. I listened to your story and ye promised to listen tae mine." Mary smoothed her palms over her skirts. There were some things that made sense to her in this world, and some things that didn't. Audrina, Maeve, whoever the woman was or what she called herself, was a mystery. But there was something she was absolutely certain of, and that was her daughter-in-law's purity of heart. Mary had sensed it the moment they discovered she was a woman under all that mud. She knew without a shadow of a doubt that she had endured things that were inexplicable. She wanted to show her that, even if her story made no sense to her, it was alright, because it made sense to someone, somehow and that was what mattered.

CHAPTER 11

A udrina fell silent as Mary continued. She would listen to Mary out of respect for a woman who had been exceedingly kind to her.

"Now, as I was sayin,' I believe ye think t'is real and what's more important t'is tha' sometimes the mind is a funny thing and sees things in a different way than most. Do ye ken wha' I'm sayin?"

Audrina nodded, and Mary continued.

"Now, ye think t'is all real, and I believe t'is real and sometimes, when a person has tae believe in something so strongly, it therefore makes it real."

Audrina understood what she was saying. Her grandfather had been a staunch believer in God, and he brought Audrina up to go to church and worship and be a devout Christian and then when she had become an adult, she decided as she learned about more denominations and religions, that the God that was real, was whatever God that particular person believed in. So, for her, she called him God, where as other people may have called him Bhudda, Allah, or any other name of their particular religion. She believed there was some higher power and everyone who believed in that, called him or her, something different. As an adult she came to realize, it wasn't important what he was called, what was important was the person's beliefs. That was what Mary was trying to say to her now.

"Ok, I understand what you are saying, Mary," she said softly.

Mary nodded and patted her hand again and continued, "Aye, so if I ken yer story, what I take from it tis, ye lost yer family at a young age. Well, that lines up with the likes of our Maeve. Her family was sent to the Heavens when a plague hit them. I'd known her mam when we was wee babies, and so she came tae live w'it us. She and Colin found each other and fell in love. Och and it was a sweet love t'was. The sun rose and shone on the likes o'Colin and Maeve. Maeve was such a sweet lass. Always lookin' after the wee ones about the castle. She was a healer, like yerself and was always mixin' brews and poultices. Some called her a witch, but nay, she was too kind-hearted a lass tae be anything o'the like. She and Colin used tae talk fer hours and hours and when we'd have a wee celebration, aye, the pair of them would be seen dancin' until the soles o'their shoes were alight. And the love they had for each other…" Mary sighed as she remembered how sweet and innocent Maeve and Colin had been.

"What happened to them, Mary?" Audrina pressed quietly.

"What happens tae e'ry sweet couple tha' finds one another round here. Now, ye ken the Scots and the English are warring w'it each other?"

"Yes." Audrina knew they were right in the middle of it.

"Aye, ye ken it well. The English claimed rights o'er the marriage bed o'the lassies of Scotland. Prima Noctem they call it."

"Yes, I've heard of it," Audrina said quietly.

"Well, on the eve o'the wedding, the English came. They're only supposed tae ha' the one night w'it the lassie, but we'd kenned ye were lost tae the likes o'Cotswold."

"Cotswold?" Audrina asked. Her head suddenly began to swim as images flared up in her mind.

Things she didn't want to ever have to endure entered her mind and she rocked back and forth clutching her head.

"Lass? Mayhap I shouldn't be pressin' ye w'it the details."

"No, please, Mary. I'm aright. Finish the story, please." Audrina continued to clutch her head.

"Are ye sure?"

"Yes, just a bit of a headache is all. I'll be fine," Audrina told her. She sat up and smiled weakly at Mary. "I suppose you think I'm crazy," Audrina started.

"Shh, lass, tis alright. No one will think such a thing of ye. And yer wee Donald Nightingale. He must ha'been yer way o'comin' face ta face wit our wee Donal. Ye had tae save him, but ye didn't ken if we'd welcome ye back. And the farmer accosting ye? Well, I ken that was yer mind forming a way to deal wit' the terrible things Cotswold did tae ye. Ye see, lass? It all does make sense in a fash. It's just a wee bit jumbled from the truth of it all."

Audrina felt a rush of emotion the more Mary talked. She clutched her head again every time she mentioned the name Cotswold. The name invoked fear into her.

"Nay, I'll no' be pressin' ye anymore this nigh'

w'it the details. Ye're too o'er come w'it emotions, lass. Ye rest now and we'll speak on it tomorrow," Mary insisted.

Audrina stood up, wanting Mary to finish the story. She had to know what happened to Maeve, but Mary placed her hands firmly on Audrina's shoulders and pushed her back down to the bed.

"Rest now, lass."

Audrina didn't think arguing was going to do her any good anymore, so she complied, lying down on the bed. It had all been so much so quickly. The museum and the pin and falling through time. Audrina didn't think she had any more energy left in her to argue with Mary until tomorrow, but she would be sure to press her to finish the story. Mary blew out the candle on the bed side lamp and that only left a soft glow emanating from the coals on the hearth. Audrina watched her walk out the door and lock her in her room just as she had when she had been taking a bath.

Audrina quickly got out of bed and tiptoed to the door, listening for anyone who might be on the other side of it.

CHAPTER 12

Audrina listened at the door and heard the soft thud of boots coming down the hall. Mary gasped and said "Oh!" as someone intercepted her just outside the door.

"Mother, tis me, Colin. How is Maeve?" he asked in a hushed tone.

"Och, Colin. I'm afraid for the wee lass. She doesnae seem to ken who she is. She's fashed quite a story about how she came tae be in the bog, but I fear all that Cotswold has done tae her has made her lose her memory."

"How do ye mean, Mother? What has she said?" Colin asked.

"She's told quite a tale of magic and time travel and the like. She doesnae even have a glimmer of recognition in her eye when I speak yer name upon my lips. I've no doubt she's Maeve alright, but she's nae the same Maeve that was taken from us. Cotswold has broken her, lad. She's romanticized the horrors he's done tae her in this outlandish tale. The mind makes up strange things when there's naught but horror and blackness tae fill it. We'll have tae be careful w'it the lass. I'm afraid if we push her, she'll snap and do somethin' drastic. I've locked her in the room so she doesnae try tae run or hurt herself," Mary finished.

Audrina listened for further comment at the door, but only heard Colin's whispered, "Alright, Mother." Before the sounds of their footsteps receded down the hall.

She turned from the door and began pacing the length of the room in the dark. What had Cotswold done to Maeve that had been so horrible? It was certain that he had invoked the rights of Prima Noctem, but was the man so horrid he had hurt Maeve in other ways? Audrina had to find out what was going on. She had to convince someone to believe her that she was not this Maeve they were all talking about. Audrina felt like for the first time, like she finally had time to be alone with her thoughts, but what she didn't like was that they all seemed to be jumbled with the memories, no stories, that everyone was telling her about Maeve.

Audrina went to her bag that she had been carrying with her from the bog. She was certain if she could find that pin, she could somehow find answers to what was going on. She had been nothing but confused and scared since she woke up in the field and she was sure if she could just get her hands on the kilt pin one more time, she would be sent home.

Audrina searched for several minutes. She completely unpacked the back and dumped the contents on the bed. Flakes of dried mud fell on the bed and Audrina even untied the packages of food she had stolen from the farmer. She searched the dried and muddied clothes she had been wearing, and still couldn't find the pin anywhere. Audrina packed it all away and began pacing the room again. She felt the tears fall from her eyes and she swiped angrily at them as she walked around the room in circles again and again.

Audrina tried to calm herself down, but the more she let her thoughts wander about the unfairness and injustice of it all, the more she got worked up. She missed home. She missed her bed with her pictures of the pretty highland castles and the comfort of her foam mattress. Audrina missed electricity and modern commodities. She had never been a dress person and every time the skirts swished around her ankles, she kicked at them angrily. The linen was rough and scratchy, and Audrina had been itching ever since she had put it on.

The more Audrina thought about these things, the more worked up she got and the harder the tears fell. Finally, she slumped down on the bed and tossed and turned for what seemed like hours as she cried. She realized the irony of her situation. She had never been able to fall asleep without staring at her pictures of the castle, and now that she was in one of the very castles she had dreamed about, she found it foreign and uninviting.

Audrina wasn't sure when she finally cried herself to sleep. She had lost track of time through most of the day because there weren't any clocks.

She sank into oblivion and soon found herself back in the tower.

"SHE STOOD AT THE WINDOW OF THE TOWER AND *looked out over the courtyard. Cotswold*

Keep was large and English soldiers surrounded the turrets and towers and walked the long catwalks in between the lookout stations. Skirmishes from the Scots had been breaking out all over the highlands, and it was only a matter of time before the clans banded together and made a move on Cotswold Castle stood high on a hill over-looking the moors of Scotland. She could see heather rippling in waves in the sun. She had lost track of time during the journey here, there had been a hood placed over her head. She'd been thrown in the tower without a word and left to tear the cloth from her face. She'd tried the door, but of course the click had sounded when the soldiers threw her in here. Now she had the painstaking task of waiting until someone came for her. She spent the majority of the day at the window. She watched the comings and goings of the English soldiers. She watched the changing of the guards below and she watched several official looking couriers ride in and out of the gates. She had nothing to do but wait while the hours passed. Wait and think about what lie ahead that night. She'd heard rumors. They'd even reached as far as Claran Castle. It's why she had denied him for so long, not wanting to face the dreadful act that would lie ahead. But she hadn't been able to nay say to him any longer. And then they had come for her. At around lunch a small bowl of stew had been sent up. The soldier who brought it hadn't said a word to her the entire time. They hadn't even bothered with a spoon and she'd had to pick the larger chunks from it and eat it with her fingers.

She'd slurped the rest of the broth down as he sneered at her and said, "You even eat like a pig. Mark my words, he'll have you squealing like one tonight too." With that, he had left and she sat on the floor and cried.

She was so scared. She knew the first wasn't pleasant to be sure, but with a man like him? She was sure she wouldn't survive the night.

She waited out the rest of the afternoon by watching the clouds roll in. Scotland's weather always fascinated her. There could be three seasons all but in a day and sure enough, the black and gray clouds boiled in the sky with an ominous mist. Supper had been the same ordeal as lunch, but this time the soldier said nothing. She found she hadn't the stomach for the contents of the bowl anyway when he spit in it before handing it to her.

He slapped her when she knocked it aside with her hand, and he shook her hard by the shoulders screaming and spitting in her face. He left after he knocked her back against the bed and she lay there and cried for the better part of an hour. It was only when the door opened one more time and a torch was shoved into the bracket on the wall and the door slammed shut that she thought about moving. She stood up and walked over to it, examining the flame which seemed to have a hypnotic effect on her.

She jumped when she heard the first clap of thunder and she turned to see the Heavens open up. It was as if they were crying for her plight and the rain lashed against the window, dripping down onto the floor. She walked over to the window, getting sprayed in the face as she went, and she caught sight of a glimmer in the puddle on the floor. She knelt and looked at her dress which was covered in the kilt and pinned at the shoulder.

She fingered the pin and felt the words begin to rise up in her being and she hastened to unfasten the pin. She knelt in the middle of the floor and placed it in the center. She picked up the torch from the wall and went about the room, gathering candles that were but stubs of the tapers they had once been. She placed them in a circle around her and knelt in the center over the pin and began to chant. When she was done chanting, she hid the pin just as the door was slammed open. The words filled her mind, body and soul.

"Bone of my bone, flesh of my flesh, through spans of time, I cannot rest. Seek thee my kin, and pardon my sin, that I may reincarnate, and new life begin. And with this pin I shall be returned to my love, cast through the ages, by touch of mine blood, and light from sun up above."

Audrina woke with a start and realized her hand was bleeding. She sat up in bed in the early morning light and discovered she was holding the very pin that she had been dreaming about and it had pricked the pad of her thumb. She switched it to her other palm and sucked absentmindedly at her bleeding thumb until the bleeding was staunched. Her brow furrowed as she concentrated hard on remembering the dream from last night. It had been the same woman she had dreamt about in her home in San Francisco, but there had been more detail. She had lived and endured with the woman through the day preceding the night that she had placed the curse on this very pin.

Audrina knew the pin was important somehow. She had frantically searched her things just last night trying to find it because she was sure it was the key to the answers she had been looking for. She remembered because she had cried herself to sleep not being able to remember where she had put it. She assumed it had been lost to the bog when she jumped in and saved little Donal, but here it was, clutched in the palm of her hand.

Audrina examined it more closely and rubbed her thumb over the waves of the silver river. When her thumb passed over the carnelian gem that represented the sun, she was sure she brushed dried mud from the gem's surface. She couldn't remember when it had fallen from her pocket, but it must have fallen in the bog if there was mud on it. As her thumb passed over the gem, Audrina had a flash go through her mind of the woman's words.

"Bone of my bone, flesh of my flesh, through spans of time, I cannot rest. Seek thee my kin, and pardon my sin, that I may reincarnate, and new life begin. And with this pin I shall be returned to my love, cast through the ages, by touch of mine blood, and light from sun up above."

THE PROMISE THAT THE CHANT MEANT WAS THAT she, the woman and the kilt pin would someday return to her love. *"Well,"* Audrina thought, *"One thing's for certain, this kilt pin certainly returned from nowhere. Is it possible that Maeve too, has reincarnated from another time and place to be returned to her love?"*

CHAPTER 13

A udrina sat on the bed holding the pin and rocking back and forth. Her idea was just too preposterous. *Reincarnation doesn't exist and that's that.* There was no way that the chant was real. It was all just a sad, scary nightmare and it was her brain's way of coping with the outlandishness of everything that had happened. Audrina could accept that she had traveled back in time. She was here, living it. She assumed it had something to do with science and somewhere, someone had invented the process to time travel and she had been the innocent bystander to be sucked up into the mechanics and theories of it all and, BAM! Here she was. What Audrina couldn't come to grips with was the idea of magic and reincarnation and all that willy nilly stuff. It didn't exist. And the more

Audrina thought about it, the worse her headache got.

She sat on the bed rocking back and forth, trying to sort out in her mind what was real and what wasn't. She didn't hear the door open and shut, and when someone cleared there throat, she jumped letting out a scream.

"Och, lass, I'm sorry. I didnae mean tae scare ye," Colin said gently.

"Colin. What…what are you doing here?" she asked.

"I came tae check on ye," he admitted a bit sheepishly.

"Why?" she blurted before she could stop herself.

"Because, lass, it doesnae matter what ye call yerself, yer still me wife and I'm worried about ye. Ye cried out in yer sleep last night and ye was cryin' I thought ye'd shed the last drop o'tears fro yer eyes a'fore ye went tae sleep, but ye still cried aft' as well," he stated simply.

Audrina was touched by his simple admission. She hadn't had anyone be concerned about her well-being since her grandfather had been alive. Colin must have been standing outside her door the entire night, she realized. He had been watching over her the whole night. She felt tears prick the backs of her eyes and she blinked rapidly so she wouldn't cry, but not before Colin hadn't noticed.

"Och, lass. Doonae cry. I'll not let anyone harm ye again." He took a step toward her, but she flinched on the bed as he drew near. The hand he held out as if he was going to touch her, dropped to his side and he looked desperately at her. "I mean it, lass. You'll ne'er be harmed by my hand or any other I command. E'ry man and woman at Claran Castle is here tae see to yer welfare. You'll be looked after. I promise ye."

"You're lord of the castle, right?" Audrina seized upon the opportunity to change the subject.

"Aye. My uncle passed last year and as he had no kin save fer me and Alisdair. As the eldest, I took the title Laird and have been lookin' after the MacClaran kinfolk e'er since." He walked to the window and looked out over the courtyard which was cast in an ethereal glow from the pale morning light. Audrina studied his profile and watched as the emotions passed across his face as he got caught up in the memory of times past.

"Tell me, about them. Your kin I mean. Tell me about your uncle and your childhood," she whispered softly.

Colin blinked at her in surprise. "Ye want me tae talk about us, lass?" he asked.

She nodded, not elaborating further and denying that she had no memories of them as children. But he thought it over for a moment and then turned back to the window.

"Aye, I remember the day ye rode through those gates sitting astride the great stallion Beastie. We called him McFarland, because we'd long since been warring with the Farland clan. We've since set aside our differences in lieu of a common enemy, the English, but the Farland clan chieftain was said tae be a great fearsome man. So, we named the stallion aft' the man himself. Only Uncle Dougal was able tae ride the creature. Some said t'was because he'd bested the Farland himself in a one on one duel, but there was naught amongst the soldiers who could sit astride the beast, but more than a moment's passing. But there ye were. All bundled up in linens and wrapped in the MacClaran tartan against the cold, sittin' in front of Uncle Dougal. I remember, I came runnin' down the steps o'the keep, brandishing a wee sword at ye and screamin' "Och, ye'll no' be infiltrating me castle, ye wee scampie!"

Uncle Dougal and the other men laughed and

ruffled my hair as they passed. They left ye standin' there in the courtyard, lookin' scared and lonely. Mother was still upstairs tendin' to Alisdair and you and I had a standoff we did. You untangled yerself from the tartan and threw it upon the ground in a fit like and ye marched yer sweet-self up tae me and put yer hands on yer hips and said, 'Aye, and who's goin' tae stop me? The likes of you?'

"Well, I didnae ken what tae do w'it such a brash and brazen wee lass and so I followed ye up the steps. Just a'fore we marched into the great hall, I realized yc'd left yer tartan lyin' on the ground and I ran back down and fetched it fer ye. Ye waited fer me at the top o'the steps and just as I was aboot tae crest them, I tripped on the tartan and went sprawlin' in a heap at yer feet. O' course, we was jest kids, nigh' goin' on six or seven I ken it. I cut my chin open and t'was bleedin' somethin' fierce. Ye took one look at me as I lay there cryin' and the sweetest expression came upon yer wee face and ye knelt beside me and began yer fussin'. Ye cooed o'er me until Mam found us sittin' on the steps together, chattin' away and talkin' about all the new places I was goin' tae take ye tae explore. Ye'd pressed the hem of yer wee apron tae me bleedin' chin and when Mam found us, ye asked for the poultices and bandages because ye were goin' tae fix me up jest right. We became thick as thieves, we did. Chasin' after one another through the years and growin' up together. T'wasn't until last year I finally convinced ye tae marry me. Everyone knew t'was only a matter of time, but yer a stubborn lass, ye ken?" he finished his story of how they'd met.

Audrina rose from the bed and walked over to the window and peered down at the courtyard with him. She could just picture a young boy and girl chasing after each other and raising all kinds of hell together that caused a ruckus. She was certain if Maeve was as determined to get back to her love as the dream and the chant suggested, then the two of them must have been deeply in love.

Audrina looked at the steps of the keep and smiled. His story was heartwarming. Maeve, a little girl with no family and no friends standing up to the bold Colin, would have been a sight to see. She was glad Maeve had been a healer like herself. It gave her a strange sense of kinship to the woman and she felt so deeply for the sorrow Colin must have been feeling at losing her. So much so that he was willing to believe that she, a stranger, was that very same woman. It was confusing and hurt her head to think about it, but she shook her head and walked away from the window. It would be all too easy to forget reality and sink willingly into the embrace of this family's welcome arms. But Audrina was still too confused and too shocked to be able to let go of all of the events that had transpired over the last forty-eight hours.

She paced the small room, stopping once more to look at the likeness on the bedside table. The woman staring back at her seemed so vivid in contrast to the others.

"Do ye no' remember it all, Maeve?" Colin asked from behind her.

She turned to stare at him.

"Do ye no' remember the way we'd laugh and jest w'it one another. We shared our hopes and dreams and we told each other everything. Have ye no memory at all, lass? I loved ye and ye loved me from the very day ye set foot on Claran grounds. Right in that courtyard. We'd chase one another through the fen. I taught ye tae ride and ye taught me tae heal scraped knees and hornet stings. Can ye at least try tae remember? Och, please, lass?" Colin beseeched her.

Audrina screwed up her face in concentration and then her hand flew to her forehead as she caught a flash of a little girl's laughter as a boy chased her through a field shouting, 'I'm gonnae get ye, Maeve! Ye're mine, ye hear? Nary any o'the other laddies can have ye, ye belong tae me!' The little girl's red hair flounced behind her as she ran away giggling. 'Ye cannae catch me, Colin MacClaran!' she shouted back at him.

Audrina felt her head swirl and her eyes went unfocused in a dizzying spell. "I…Colin…I don't remember," she finally said as she sat down on the edge of the bed.

Colin looked slightly crestfallen, but nodded his head. "Tis alright, lass, I ken t'will take time." He then walked to the door and Audrina looked down at the small parcel he had placed on the bed when he had walked in.

"What's this?" she asked.

"Tis a gift, lass. T'was supposed tae be a wedding present," he said as he turned to the door. "Mayhap ye'll wear it down tae breakfast?" he asked hopefully before he turned to the door and walked out.

Audrina carefully unwrapped the package and found a carefully folded tartan in the MacClaran colors. It was a beautifully woven piece of fabric and it looked as if it had recently been dyed because the colors were pristine and had never been washed. Audrina held the fabric up in the morning light and admired the colors she had seen countless times when she had been exploring her roots with her grandfather.

She rose from the bed and wrapped the plaid around her, taking the pin from the pocket of her simple dress, and fastening the fabric in place with the pin. It somehow felt right that she had placed it there, and that feeling was one Audrina desperately craved because her life had been turned upside down. In all the confusion and chaos, a small feeling of right was most welcomed by her. She walked to the door and made her way downstairs to the great hall. The entire way down, as she passed wooden doors and stone walls, she began to wonder as she thought about the flash of the little girl and the little boy if those were her memories. She wondered what was real and what was not.

CHAPTER 14

Audrina made her way down to the great hall, and she admired the simplicity of the castle. It wasn't like any castle she had imagined. The decorations were simple enough, and practical. She noted that tapestries seemed to be the theme along the walls as she walked. She had learned from her grandfather that they were used to keep the cold at bay. Stone walls offered very little insulation and the draft in the winter months would cause many Scotsman to take ill and in many cases, die from their sickness.

Audrina knew this to have some merit as she was a practitioner in medicine, but she marveled at the intricate designs woven into the tapestries as she passed. She wondered at how much more character was detailed into the hangings than modern wall paper or paint. It seemed to her that people of the modern world could change the appearance of their walls if they so choose, because it was a commodity and so the necessity of beauty and design was irrelevant. Here, however, Audrina discovered the everlasting beauty came with the intricacies of the designs. They were so minute and finite, that one could spend days admiring them and be lost in discovering all the little secrets woven into the fabric.

Audrina found herself lost in such a transfixed way, until someone cleared their throat behind her. She jumped and turned on her heel at the sound and found herself face to face with Alisdair, Colin's younger brother.

"Apologies, mi'lady," he said quietly. "I didnae mean tae frighten ye."

Audrina gave him a small smile. "It's alright," she said.

"I ken ye like the look of the weave?" he asked, gesturing to the tapestry.

"Yes, it's very pretty," she responded. They fell into an awkward silence, staring at one another.

"Well, I suppose we could have one brought tae yer room for ye tae look at all ye like, Maeve," he said to her.

Audrina felt her spirit fall. She was just starting to feel some semblance of normalcy, even in the small task of admiring what would have been to her, a piece of ancient artwork in modern times. She realized Alisdair meant to please Maeve and that he was still treating her fragile, like she might break.

"That would be nice," she responded.

"I don't suppose, ye've lost yer way and need an escort down tae breakfast do ye?" he asked hopefully.

"That would be lovely thank you," she responded again. She figured he probably wasn't going to leave her in peace until she was safely seen between rooms, and not left to wander about the castle on her own.

She walked beside him until they reached the stairs, and then Alisdair took the lead, holding a torch high so she could see as she descended into the great hall.

When she got to the landing, she looked around the room which was packed with people. Everyone looked in her direction as she began walking beside Alisdair again, toward the head table. A sea of faces looked back at her and they all began whispering to one another and pointing to her. Audrina walked closer to Alisdair as they approached the table and she was grateful to see an empty seat beside Mary.

"Mornin', lass," Mary said as she scooted over so Audrina could sit down. "Have a good sleep then?"

She handed Audrina a tray of breads which Audrina took gratefully. She wasn't sure what was on the meat tray, and she didn't think she could stomach finding out.

"Yes, thank you." Audrina said. She cast a look in Colin's direction as he was seated to her left. He raised an eyebrow, but spared her the embarrassment of having to explain her nightmare and crying in her sleep.

"Do ye naught eat yer kippers, lass?" Mary asked her, handing her the tray of meat.

"Umm, no thank you." She waved her hand at it and Mary looked at her like she wanted to place a hand over her forehead to see if she was feeling alright.

"Tatties then?" Mary was obviously trying to get her to eat, deeming her as sickly.

Fortunately, Audrina recognized tatties as the word for potatoes, and she gratefully accepted the plate and took a helping for herself. She handed the tray to Colin without a word and turned her attention back to her own plate.

It wasn't long before she had begun to dig in and eat, that someone approached the bench. A plump woman who Audrina recognized from the day before came to the bench, wringing her hands in her apron. Her ample bust jiggled in her dress, and Audrina realized all the men at the table except Colin, were staring at her chest instead of listening to what she had to say.

"Och, had I ken t'was ye yesterday, Lady Maeve, I'd hae taken ye straight tae his Lairdship. Tis good tae see ye've been found and I'd thank his Laird tae remember auld Maudie took care o'his lady at the pub yesterday." Maudie curtsied as best as her plump bottom would allow for her to bend in her dress.

Audrina really wished she hadn't because she was in danger of falling out of her dress. She nodded at Maudie and was grateful when she returned to her seat, because her cold sores on the sides of her mouth were really off-putting, and Audrina had a sneaking suspicion she knew which diseases Maudie had contracted when she "took care" of people who came into her bar.

Audrina was just picking at the berries she had

put on her plate when another person approached the table. It was one of the men who had accompanied Colin into the forest yesterday to save Donal. He was older than the rest with silver hair and a silvered mustache and beard.

"Tis good tae see ye hale and hearty, lass. I cannae thank the Lord Almighty tha' yer home safe. I remember the day we rode in w'it Dougal MacClaran w'it ye sittin' astride his horse. Ye were just a wee lass then, but look at ye now. Back home and safe w'it yer man and out o'the clutches o'the English swine!" He spit into the rushes on the floor at his feet. No one seemed to mind that he had done such a thing. When he called them the English Swine, a loud, raucous cheer went up through the tables.

Audrina didn't know how to respond to such a proclamation, so she merely nodded. It seemed to go on like this, all through breakfast and Audrina would pause and listen to whatever the person had to say to welcome her home. It appeared as if her return to the castle had made its way around the castle and she was a mix between somewhat of a hero for escaping Cotswold and viewed as an invalid because more than once, someone wished her a well and speedy recovery.

Through it all, Mary and Colin said nothing. Mary mostly because she was after Donal to sit still and eat his breakfast. It appeared as if he was having more fun flicking berries toward Maudie, and seeing if he could land one in her ample cleavage. This caused the dogs who were great shaggy beasts to emerge from under the tables and rest half the distance between the head table and Maudie's table. Audrina thought the dogs looked savage and untamed and she wasn't in a hurry to get to know them, until Donal held his plate under the table and one approached, wagging its tail gleefully and licked the plate clean.

Audrina was shocked to see Donal had shockingly blond hair. It was so blond it was almost white. Yesterday he had been so caked in mud, she had just assumed it was brown.

As breakfast began winding down, and Mary's nerves were clearly frayed, Donal escaped her clutches and ran around the table so that he was facing her.

"I ne'er thanked ye fer savin' me yester'eve, sister," he started. It took a minute for Audrina to understand that he thought he was talking to Maeve, and that by marriage, she was his sister-in-law.

"It's alright, Donal. I'm just glad I got there in time," she said quietly.

The boy grinned and continued, "Of course, ye ken I was almost out'o the bog by the time ye arrived. There I was, ridin' Fergus aft a wild boar tha' had been aft' the food stores. I mounted the steed and chased aft the wee beastie as it was squealin' and snortin' somat fierce ye ken?"

Audrina smiled at him.

His face lit up impishly as he realized she wasn't going to nay say his story. He continued with a mischievous grin on his face, "Och aye, the beastie ran across the log and I urged Fergus onward, but then, out o' the bog, rose a great and monstrous beastie! Tis said tae be the kin o'the loch monster. T'was covered in mire and much and it roared somat fierce at Fergus and I. Fergus reared his head and tossed me into the mire like a rag doll, but I wasnae afraid! Nay! I rose up and brandished me sword and cursed at the creature. But the beast kenned I was alone then, and it raised its mighty tentacle and came crashing down around me. Water and mud sprayed toward the heavens, ye ken? But I held fast to me sword."

As Donal told his story, he captivated the audience with his tale as he gestured with his arms about the great and powerful beast. He flapped his arms in the air to demonstrate the tentacles of the creature, and he struck a pose as he pretended to brandish the sword in the air. All the while, the children sitting around the benches stared at him, wild-eyed and in awe. The adults suppressed fits of laughter, but no one dared question or interrupt the Laird's little brother.

"Aye, t'was near the end o'it fer me, but I thrust at the beast w'it all my might and lanced the creature through the heart! T'was then I realized I was in the thick o'it. I couldnae grab the log that Fergus and I had tried to cross. The beastie made sure tae drag me too far off. Then ye appeared out'o the mist, like a wraith come back from the dead. Ye held out yer arms and I grasped on. But yer a woman. I could tell by the way ye'd wrapped the kilt and cloth about ye. And e'ery one knows a woman doesnae ha' the strength o'a man. Ye fell inta the water, and I jumped and grabbed the branch, draggin' ye w'it me onto the bank with me one arm, and w'it me sword clenched between me teeth!" he finished.

Audrina clapped along with the rest of audience at his tale of heroics. She caught a glimpse of Colin's eye and the mirth shone brightly in the depths of the startling blue eyes. She looked away quickly as something fluttered in her chest. As she watched young Donal bow and raise the crowd for more clapping, she snorted to herself as she realized the irony of Scotland being the only place she could go and change out of pants in order to be more masculine. Donal's little kilt hung off his skinny torso in bunches. It would be a long time before he would grow big enough, so it didn't look like he was not only drowning in tall-tales, but material as well.

Audrina sucked in a breath. She remembered when she and Grandfather would be sitting around the fireplace. He would tuck into his old plaid armchair and sit her on his knee. He would tell her similar outlandish tales of sea monsters and knights rescuing fair ladies. The nostalgia hit her in a wave as she had the flicker of emotion that it wasn't just her grandfather, but a man, an older man with a long shaggy beard and twinkling blue eyes the color of Colin's. Perhaps it was Colin's father? But that couldn't be right. She thought maybe it was his Uncle Dougal, the man who came to rescue her, Maeve, from Skye and brought her back to the keep. She had the strangest sense that he too, would tell outlandish tales to sleepless little girls with red hair.

Audrina smiled into her porridge and finished eating. All of the talking and reminiscing, well-wishing and sympathetic looks had made her tired. She decided the best thing she needed was a little nap where her sleep had been so disturbed.

CHAPTER 15

A udrina decided to take the long way back to her chambers. Although she was tired and could use a bit of rest, she had been cooped up in the chamber for most of the day yesterday and all night. She decided to take a nice long walk, and then having a mid-morning nap would be just what she needed to clear her thoughts. She walked around the great hall for a spell, occasionally being interrupted on her walk and hailed a greeting in passing. It seemed the whole keep was ecstatic at her return, although she could have done without the sympathetic smiles and the well-wishes for a speedy recovery. That implied that she was ill, and she certainly didn't feel ill. She knew they all assumed she had memory loss, but she honestly wasn't sure what was real and what wasn't anymore.

As Audrina walked, she discovered the kitchens which were bustling with activity in preparation for the evening meal. She felt like she was just in the way as the activity stopped when she entered. She didn't want to be a pest and it seemed every person in the kitchen asked how they could be of service, and that meant they were neglecting whatever chores they had to attend to. Audrina left the kitchen which was on a sub-level and dug underground. She walked back up the narrow dark stairs, careful not to trip on her gown, and made her way back around the great hall again. It was strange to her to think about the two-dimensional pictures back in her bedroom. In some respects, Castle Claran was huge and as grand as she envisioned them to be from her pictures. In other areas, such as the staircases, the castle seemed squashed, dark and dank.

Audrina tried various doors and if they were locked, she left them alone and if they were opened, she took a peek inside. A lot of them were simply storage chambers for either food, goods, or weapons. She found a few bedchambers, but she quickly ducked out, not wanting to intrude on anyone's personal space. She found a small door at the back of the great hall that wasn't locked, but when she pushed the door open, she discovered the hinges creaked and the spider webs up above still clung to the door. It obviously hadn't been opened in a very long time.

Audrina had been acutely aware of someone's presence behind her as she explored the castle. She stepped through the door and hid behind it and waited a hare's breath before she heard the soft rustle of footsteps pass through the door.

"Hello," she said quietly. The person behind her let out a shocked and terrified yelp.

"What are ye doin'?" young Donal demanded once he recovered himself.

"Just looking around a bit before I head back upstairs. Why are you following me?" she countered.

"Erm, because Colin said yer naught t'be left ter yerself," was Donal's reply.

"So he wants me guarded so I won't run away?" Audrina demanded.

He face flushed as she became annoyed. "Aye and nay. He's worried about ye is all. He doesnae want ye tae do anything foolish. Tis wha' he has me fer anyway." He grinned at her.

Audrina felt herself soften a little. She liked Donal's mischievous ways. "Where's your mother? I imagine she's looking for you," Audrina replied.

"Aye she is. I gave her the slip. She's always chasin' aft' me. But I go where I likes and I do as I please." He puffed up his skinny chest a little.

"Yeah? And does doing as you please ever get you in trouble like it did yesterday?" Audrina asked.

"Aye sometimes. But Mam is sickly-like. She's always gettin' the maids tae chase aft' me. But I'm gettin' better at findin' ways tae get away from 'em!"

Audrina laughed at his audacity. "Why is your mam sick?" she asked.

"She didnae think she could have me after Alisdair. She was barren fer ten years. Then aft' I was born, she became a widow when Da died. Uncle Dougal had been lookin' aft' us as Da was always away on trips fer him and such. Then Uncle Dougal, her brother passed, and Colin became Laird, so she's always been lady o'the house. Now with ye come back tae us, I suspect she'll finally rest a wee bit."

"Yes, that is if you give her a chance to rest. I have a feeling your temperament is rather impish, and you give her quite the run for her money,"

Audrina retorted, still laughing. She always knew widows in the early centuries found a lot of hardships, but Mary had certainly had her run of the mill. In some ways Donal's youth and vivaciousness would keep her young as she chased after him. In other ways, it probably wore her out. "And what about you? Have you ever been sick?" Audrina grilled him. She could feel her own motherly instincts kick in where Donal was concerned and she would be certain to help Mary chase after him if necessary.

"Aye, I've had me fair share o'bouts of the fever, but I always pull through," he told her.

Audrina nodded and then turned back to the stairs. The torches in those hallways weren't lit. "Where does this go?" she asked.

"Tae the tower," Donal replied.

"Yes, I suspected as much, but what's up there?" she asked.

"Well, I ken it was where ye did yer healin' and such. Colin closed the door when ye didnae come back. He never expressly forbade anyone from goin' up there, but n'ane ha' e'er gone up there in o'er a year."

"Go and fetch me a torch. I want to go see what's up there," Audrina told him.

He scampered off and came back within minutes with a long torch and Audrina made her way up the steps. She brushed past cobwebs and stepped carefully around scurrying creatures. The first few startled her until she summoned her courage after Donal laughed at her from behind.

When she reached the top of the stairs, she pushed open the door to the tower. It was a round circular room like the one in her dream, but this one was full of benches and tables with bottles of various medicinal properties. She picked up a few bottles and read them. This must have been where Maeve had practiced her healing abilities for the people of Claran Castle. She felt her nursing instincts kick in and she began categorizing the bottles and she even organized one of the benches. She liked this room, it suited her. It made her apprehension about exploring towers lessen, if only slightly.

When she was done, she decided it was time to return to her room and have that nap. As she and Donal descended the steps and pushed through the door to the great hall, if Colin witnessed her leaving the tower as he was walking in for a bit of lunch, he didn't say anything.

Audrina climbed the steps at the opposite end

of the great hall and made her way back to her room. One of the maids was just leaving as she entered and she had left some food for her to eat. This time she noticed there was very little meat on the tray, and they had favored breads, cheeses and fruits for her. She sat at the table and began eating and then she heard a knock at the door.

"Come in!" she called.

Mary entered the room carrying some more fresh linens which she set on the bed.

"I see ye've explored our home a wee bit. Donal was verra excited ye took him along on yer adventure. I thank ye for lookin' aft' him."

"Of course, it was my pleasure, Mary. Thank you for the linens," she said.

"Aye, tis no trouble, dear. Anyway, I thought perhaps if yer ready, we'd finish the story." She looked at Audrina as if to gauge her mental stability.

"Yes, of course. Please tell me what happened to Maeve and Colin."

Mary sat down on the edge of the bed while Audrina ate. She offered her some, but she waved a wrinkled hand and continued.

"Alright, as I was saying last eve, as Prima Noctem dictates, the English are supposed tae take a wee lass fer one night and one night only. Colin and Maeve were married in secret, and that's the reason Maeve held off fer so long sayin' aye t'our Colin. She didnae want tae go tae the English. So they decided tae be wed in the middle o'the night. But Cotswold, his spies run thick as thieves. The soldiers came just aft' the vows were said, and they dragged wee Maeve off tae Cotswold Castle. Now, the English are supposed tae bring the lass back tae her husband the day after the wedding night. But Cotswold didn't. Tis rumored he ha' his way w'it the lassies and does unspeakable evils t'them. We waited naught e'en a fortnight and then Colin went tae collect ye himself. Cotswold said ye'd run off, but we knew he'd been so rough w'it ye that he'd broken ye. T'was not the first time he'd done it tae a lass. Over the last few years, several o'the lassies ha'gone missin. T'wasn't until ye wandered in tae the bog and rescued wee Donal that we knew ye had been kept alive all this time. Och, lass, I cannae imagine the horrors ye've faced at the hands of Cotswold this past year. Tis no wonder ye've fashed a tale as such. I wouldnae put it past Cotswold tae dump ye in a coo field once he was done w'it ye. And then, tae cope w'it the horror, ye disguised yerself, kenning ye were in disgrace or some such like."

Audrina sat listening to the tale in horror. She couldn't imagine such a horrible thing happening to Maeve. She couldn't imagine such a horrible thing happening to her. But what was truly horrible, was she couldn't wrap her brain around how it had happened to her, or Maeve, or somehow, she knew it wasn't her, but it was Maeve. Audrina felt hot tears begin to slip down her cheeks.

CHAPTER 16

"It's not true! It can't be true!" Audrina stood and began pacing the room. She wept uncontrollably as the confusion and the nightmare seemed to mesh with her reality. Flashes of her nakedness and shame filtered through her mind. She palmed the kilt pin and heard the chant one more time as she watched as a hand, her hand place it behind the stone in the wall. She heard a cold laugh in her head and a scream of pain the likes of which she had never heard, even as a trauma nurse.

Audrina clutched her head when she heard the scream. "It's not true, it's not true!" she chanted over and over, as if saying the words would take the images from her head. The more the flashes and bits of the nightmare that entered her mind came, the more hysterical she became.

Mary rose and went to her, trying to remove her hands from her head. "Och, I ken ye've been through a terrible ordeal now, Maeve, but lass, as I said, I believe ye. Ye've fashed a tale to cope w'it the horrors, but lass, tis all true."

"No!" Audrina shouted at her. "Get away from me! You're lying!" she cried. Great racking sobs took over her body as she tried to bury the images from her mind.

She began to rip and claw at the linens on the bed, in a fit of hysterics. "This isn't real! It can't be real! I'm dreaming, and I need to wake up!" she screamed.

Mary gasped as she clawed the kilt pin from her tartan and let the fine material fall to the floor. She ran to the window and threw the pin out the window into the courtyard.

"Och lass, I'm sorry. I'm verra sorry. I didnae mean tae upset ye so!" Mary cried. "Please forgive me, lass, I didnae mean tae cause ye more pain," she begged.

Audrina threw herself onto the bed and cried uncontrollably. When Mary went to her to put her arms around her, she jerked away and stood in the corner, sobbing hysterically.

A few moments later they both heard the

unmistakable sound of boots running through the hallway, and Audrina cried even harder. The sound of the boots reminded her of the sound of the boots on the stone steps from her nightmare. They drew closer and closer and she became more hysterical. Mary continued to plead with her to calm down, but it was to no avail.

The door to the chamber was thrown open and Colin strode in, his sword in his hand.

"What's happened?" he demanded. "Ha'e ye been attacked?"

The sight of the sword upset Audrina more. It was too real for her. The castle and the gowns and the swords. But in a way, it was all too much. She couldn't get her emotions under control and she didn't hear as Mary briefly explained to Colin what had happened, or when the woman had slipped from the chamber.

Colin strode over to Audrina who shrieked and tried to pull away, until he put the sword back in the scabbard and gathered her in his arms. She struggled against him for a time, but he walked backwards until his knees bumped the bed and then he sank down onto it and dragged her down with him. She cried into his chest for a time, but with every inhale of his masculine scent, her emotions and nerves calmed a little bit more, and then a little bit more.

Audrina began to hiccup as she lay in Colin's arms. He whispered to her and kissed the top of her head. He sang songs to her in a tongue and language she didn't recognize. She knew it must be Gaelic, she had heard her grandfather turn a phrase or two when he was emotional or excited about something.

Her hiccups turn to soft sighs as she lay in his arms, and she was fairly certain she dozed off a time or two, as she had been so restless the night before.

Colin seemed to take it all in stride and whatever he had been doing, was long forgotten because he made no indication that he wanted to be anywhere else. He continued to hold her and speak to her, even when she dozed a little. She'd wake with a start and he could feel her heart flutter in remembrance as realization came crashing down around her again and he wanted to be right there to reassure her it was all going to be alright.

Audrina turned in his arms and looked at the ceiling frowning.

"What is it, lass?" he asked softly.

"There are no pictures," she said just as softly.

Her voice was, and she sounded nasally from all the crying, but he didn't seem to mind. He tucked a strand of wayward red hair back behind her ear.

"What do ye mean?" he asked.

She decided to tell him. They all thought she was mentally fragile anyway, and she needed an outlet.

"In my room, in San Francisco," she began.

"Ye mean the place in yer head ye escaped?" He looked down at her.

"Will you do something for me, Colin?" she asked looking up into his blue eyes.

"Aye, anything, lass," he murmured.

"Can you please just pretend?"

"Pretend?"

"Yes, just make believe. You know, pretend like it's real, because it's very real to me and I know your mother has been extremely kind to me since I've arrive, everyone has really; it's just that, no one has truly believed me. I need someone to pretend, like it's all real."

Colin sighed, and she could see him clearly thinking over if he should indulge her or not.

"Alright, lass, I'll pretend. Tell me about your San Francisco." The words sounded foreign on his lips, but he gave her a soft kiss on the forehead, like somehow his kiss could heal her mentally if she was permitted to get it all out.

"Well, back in my room in San Francisco, I had pictures up on the ceiling. They were pictures that my grandfather cut out for me. Most of them were faraway places, here in Scotland you see. There was Cotswold Castle and Claran Castle and the Isle of Skye. There was a picture of a thistle and some highland cows, or as you say, coos. And the thing about these pictures is, they always helped me sleep. I used to have nightmares after my mom passed away. So, when my grandfather took me in, he placed them on the ceiling, so I could look at them before I went to sleep and dream about faraway places. We would explore our ancestry together, because we are direct descendants of your Maeve's sister, Catriona. She had a daughter who was taken away by Catriona's husband's family and I know that Maeve was brought here to you. I don't know what happened to their other sister, Moira, but I know a plague came over the Isle of Skye and wiped out most of the population. Anyway, Grandfather and I would talk for hours and hours about the Catriona James' descendants. He never included the story of you and Maeve, maybe he thought it was too sad. But the pictures made me yearn for places that I had never been to. There's a word for it, several in fact, wanderlust or fernweh. I've always yearned to come to Scotland and explore the pictures. But what I find most disturbing is, even though I am in the very castle of one of my pictures, I can't sleep because I stare at the ceiling and, all I see are stones." She fell silent and Colin didn't say a word for a long moment.

After a minute he said, "Did ye e'er think, lass, that ye've dreamed up these pictures just so ye could fall asleep?"

He wasn't judging her, he was asking a simple honest question, but it confused her. She'd had so much trouble discerning reality from what a dream was lately, his question was legitimate and fair.

"I don't know what I dream about anymore," she admitted truthfully.

"Well, what if ye painted me a picture w'it yer words about yer, San Francisco?" he asked her.

She turned her head up to him to study his face. He was asking a sincere question and she didn't feel like he was only entertaining her fanciful imaginations, so she told him. She told him about the Golden Gate Bridge and the cable cars. She told him of the hilly streets and looking out onto the bay. She told him about the redwood trees that she would go explore when she was a child and she told him of her fondest memories of her grandfather. When he sensed a touch of sadness in her voice about her grandfather, he asked, "What was his name?"

"Argus," she answered.

"That was the name ye gave us when ye were havin' us believe ye were a wee laddie," he commented.

"Yes. It was. He was very proud of the fact that he is a James from the clan James in Scotland. It meant a lot to him."

"Aye, I ken that. We Scots are a proud people."

"Yes, I ken that too." She tried his words out on her tongue.

It seemed to please him because Colin let out a chuffed breath and she continued her story. She came to the harder parts about working all the time and the death and trauma she saw at the hospital. He squeezed her a little tighter as she told him about losing Donald Nightingale. It hit close to home for him as well.

When she was finished telling him about her story, he remained quiet for a moment, and then he said, "If ye fancy bein' a healer tae the people, the tower and the stores are yers. It might take a while fer the people tae come tae ye, they think ye've had a bad spell and yer no' quite right in the head, but once they see ye heal a few people up a bit, they'll be flockin' tae ye like geese."

Audrina felt immense gratitude at his generosity. "Thank you, Colin. I know that place was special to your Maeve."

He blinked at her and she realized he still thought she was Maeve, she just had a very skewed vision of herself at the moment, but he didn't argue with her and she was content to remain in his arms on the bed.

CHAPTER 17

A udrina and Colin remained lying on the bed for a while longer. She was beginning to wonder if he was going to let her up, but he seemed reluctant to let her go, even for the briefest moment whilst she shifted on the bed. What shocked her even more as she calmed down while she was talking to him, was that she felt safe and secure in the comfort of his arms. She was almost reluctant to get up herself. But as the morning passed and the sun rose high in the sky, Audrina decided she couldn't remain cooped up in the chamber all day.

She wiggled her way free and after a few moments of struggling to keep her on the bed, Colin let her go and she stood looking down at him.

He was so big, and his muscles flexed as he stretched out and watched her.

Audrina bit her lip and then stammered, "Thank you for listening to me. Umm, you didn't have to, I'm sure you had other things to be doing. I didn't think I was going to stop crying once I had started and, well, you ahh, made it better."

She realized she was babbling and he smiled up at her for the first time. It was devastatingly beautiful as it cracked the hardened visage of his face that was always steeled into a mask of impassivity or determined concentration. She was pleased to note that his teeth were shockingly white and clean, and she was grateful that unlike many of the townspeople she had encountered, he seemed to have a grasp on the importance of personal hygiene. She noticed the overall issue was less of an issue here in the keep than it was out in the town.

Audrina continued to stare down at Colin, who slowly sat up on the bed as she watched him. Audrina took a step back, concerned he was going to embrace her again, but he left his hands at his side so as not to startle her.

Very quietly he asked, "Are ye sure ye doonae remember me, lass? The way ye've looked at me just now…" he trailed off.

Audrina thought for a moment and then said, "No, Colin. I don't remember you." His face looked crestfallen and for some reason she couldn't stand to see him so sad, so she said, "But, I did throw myself into the mud in the bog to save your brother, so there must be some part of me, something I don't understand that is going on."

Colin looked at her thoughtfully and reached out to her, but she backed away quickly toward the door. She was afraid if he touched her again, she would fall back into his arms and not want him to let her go. Audrina didn't know if she had just lied to Colin or not, or even more disturbingly, if there was something else going on, and suddenly, she couldn't stand to be in the same cramped space with him. The chamber walls felt like they were closing in around her and so she turned to the door, yanking it open and fled.

She ran down the stairs and entered the great hall. Mary stood up in a hurry, looking concerned.

"Lass, what is it? What's wrong?"

But Audrina didn't answer her. She turned to the doors of the great hall and although she couldn't open them by herself, she seized upon the opportunity to slip past Alisdair and flee out into the courtyard in the bright sunshine.

Audrina ran as hard and as fast as she could. She was sweating by the time she reached the gates across the moat and she wasn't hampered when she fled through the open doors. The gates were always kept open to the public to come and go as they pleased during the day. They were rarely closed with the exception of nighttime and the potential for an attack.

Audrina ran down the narrow path, not minding where she was going, and she kept running, through the muddy streets of the town, soaking her slippers.

She heard the thud of boots behind her and she pushed through the crowds as she kept running. Shouts of alarm rang in her ears, but she ignored them as she barreled past and found the narrow path that she had traveled into town on.

As athletic as Audrina was, it didn't take her long to sprint along the path toward the field where she had woken up in. She knew she ran the risk of running into the farmer again, but she didn't care. She had to get to that field and find answers. She couldn't stand not knowing what was real and what wasn't anymore.

She heard Colin shout behind her, but she

didn't slow down. "Maeve, lass, stop!" he shouted, and she kept on running.

When she got to the field, she targeted the area by sight that she thought she might have landed. She knew it was along the tree line at the back of the field, so she sprinted across the field. She dodged cow patties and potholes and she tugged at her dress, ripping it a little as it became snared in a patch of nettles. She could feel her hair plastered to her neck and she loathed the hot summer sun as it beat down on her back.

When she reached the spot that she thought might be where she had traveled through time, she stopped and spun in circles. This had to be the place, she just knew it. But how had she gotten here? Why was this place special?

Colin ran astride her and for the first time he looked genuinely upset with her. "Och lass, wha' the bloody hell do ye think yer doin'? Ye've given us all a righ' scare ye have!" he thundered.

She lost her temper with him too. "This is it! This is the place! Why isn't it working? This is where I fell, and this is where I woke up with a stupid cow licking my face! That one!" She pointed to the same lumbering cow with the white patch on its long brown shaggy fur. It swished its tail and had the audacity to moo at them.

"Lass, do ye hear yerself? O'course this is the field ye collapsed in. No one's denyin' tha's the way it happened, but look o'er there." He pointed to the far end of the field. "Tha's the road that leads tae Cotswold's Castle. He most like let ye go, or maybe ye escaped and ye were so broken when ye did, ye almost made it home, but ended up collapsing in this here field!"

Audrina turned in a circle again, not willing to face the road. "I'm not lying, Colin. Please believe me, please!" she begged. "I had the pin. It was right here!"

She turned in another circle, looking for the pin until she remembered she had thrown it out the window. Colin fished in his sporran for some-thing and to Audrina's dismay, he pulled the kilt pin out.

"Ye mean this pin here, lass? Alisdair thought he was bein' attacked by the English when it nigh' hit him o'er the head when ye threw it out the window. I recognized it fer what it was and picked it up. That's when we heard a screamin' wail start up that was unholy-like. I came runnin' and found ye and me mam in yer room, havin' a go at one another."

He walked over and held the pin out to Audrina who let it fall into her upturned palm.

It felt warm to the touch, but that may have been because she'd made Colin chase her for almost a mile through the streets and through a field. She closed her palm around it and willed herself back to the museum, but nothing happened. When she opened her eyes, Colin was standing in front of her with his arms crossed and nothing less than a politely patient expression on his face. Audrina looked around as the cow ambled up to her and began nuzzling her palm again. She patted it and it mooed encouragingly at it, which only irritated her more.

"Colin…" she began, but he held up his palm.

"Now listen tae me, lass. I've heard yer story and I've listened tae ye, but tis time ye accept the fact that yer here, w'it me. I ken ye ended up in this field somehow, lass, bloody hell, e'en the bloody coo kens it, but ye cannae go runnin' off whene'er it takes yer fancy!" he thundered.

Audrina flinched, and he sighed as he realized he'd frightened her. "Och, lass, I'm verra sorry I was harsh w'it ye. But there are men who willnae be so patient w'it ye if ye cross their path. Ye're a woman and some men, like Cotswold, they…" But before he could finish his sentence, a shout rang out as someone came running up to them.

To Audrina's horror, it was the very farmer who had accosted her.

"Wha' the bloody hell do ye think yer doin?" he roared. He had clearly not forgotten she had beat him up and left him lying in the field. Or that she had stolen from him. "I swore tae me dead mam if I e'er caught ye near my coos again, lass…" he thundered. He seemed to not have noticed Colin because he was fixated on her and her red hair. He raised his fists at her until Colin stepped in front of him.

"Tha's me wife yer threatenin', man. I suggest ye remember yer place in the face of yer Laird!" he hollered at the farmer.

The farmer cursed and spat and pointed at her. "She kicked me bawbag! She struck me face! Aye, and then the wee hellion wench stole from me stores and took me clothes!" he snarled at her.

Audrina snapped at him in fury, "Well you tried to rape me! I was alone and scared in a field all by myself and you took one look at me and called me a whore! What was I supposed to do, let you have your way with me and then leave me lying there!"

Colin looked back and forth between the two of

them, his face thunderous. He turned back to the farmer and began speaking in rapid Gaelic. She understood very little, but she heard the name Cotswold, and she recognized when he pointed to the road. Then he said some more stuff and then pointed to himself. The farmer listened intently, but continued to glare at her. She glared right back and continued petting the cow.

When they were done, both men turned to her and the farmer spat one more time. This seemed to anger Colin who said, "As Laird I doonae permit the harm of the women under my care. Fer yer disgrace I'm fining ye one coo."

"Ye cannae do that! She stole from me!"

"Aye, and as we've just discussed, she wasnae in her right mind." He fished in his sporran again and pulled out a few coins dropping them on the ground at the farmer's feet. "Recompense fer the food and clothes, but the coo is the fine fer accostin' yer Laird's wife!"

The farmer seemed to mull it over a moment, but when Colin's hand went to his sword in atime old tradition of honoring his wife by battle with the offender, the farmer thought better of it and said, "Tis a fare fine, me Laird, but please see tae it that yer wee wife, stays out o'me fields!"

Colin raised his eyebrow at the man, letting him have his moment of due on the battlefield, and then turned to Audrina and took the thin rope dangling from the cow's neck.

"Come on Bessie, on w'it ye now." He slapped the rump of the cow. "Lass?" He looked at Audrina expectantly.

She sighed and followed after him, unsure of anything anymore. She hadn't proved to herself that standing in the exact spot that she had arrived at and holding the exact pin that had a spell cast on it would bring her back to her time. But as the words of the chant filled her head, she wasn't sure they were entirely wrong and that the promise for person and pin to be returned to Colin, hadn't happened. The one thing she was sure of was, she had always wanted a pet, and as the cow mooed and swished its tail happily, she finally had one.

CHAPTER 18

Audrina returned to her room under the reproachful eye of the members of the Claran household. She was exhausted and sweaty and she wasn't in the mood to answer any more questions from people. She was tired of the sympathetic looks that were cast her way and the whispered, "lost memory" or "not right in the head" that she heard everywhere she turned.

She decided to skip dinner, opting for the meal that was sent up for her from one of the maids. She didn't bother to turn away from the window when the maid came in. She did however enjoy the bath that was brought up this time. She sank into the water gratefully and enjoyed the warmth it provided as the rain lashed against the window.

The clouds had rolled in as was typical of a late summer afternoon shower in Scotland. She had said very little to Colin on the walk back to the keep, and he had let her stew in her own thoughts. He had gone off to take Bessie, or the cow, as most cows were called Bessie around here, to find a stall in the stable.

Audrina had trudged up to her room, not looking at or speaking to anyone. She felt like the chamber was a prison somehow, but a lavish one at that. Especially for this time period. But she also felt like it was a prison of her own making. No one had told her she had to come up here, yet she did anyway. She wasn't sure why, except that maybe she had still been running from something. From herself or from others, she wasn't sure.

After Audrina got out of the tub, she dried off and waited, wrapped in her shift and the tartan that Colin had brought to her the previous day. She sat by the fire and stared into it absentmindedly as the tub was hauled away and she was finally left to herself.

Audrina got up a while later and decided to just go to bed. There were no books to read and she was an avid romance reader. She wasn't sure how she felt on the romance front either. She'd always been emotionally closed off, not having many boyfriends as she worked long hours. She'd gotten used to having to be on her own after her grandfather passed. In some ways that was true when he had been still alive, because he had left her to her own devices when it came to romance and love. He himself had been a bit of a social recluse. He rarely went out or met friends and he never dated. Audrina knew very little about her grandmother except the fact that her grandfather had been deeply in love with her. When she lost the battle with cancer, it had stolen not only her grandmother's life, but a piece of her grandfather's soul as well. Maybe that was the legacy her grandfather never wanted to tell her about. Maybe that's why all record of Maeve's relationship with Colin had been stricken from the records. Maybe the pain of lost love was the curse of the James clan, and the legend that the James clan found one and only one love during their time. It would explain some things about Maeve and Colin, to be sure.

But Audrina sighed inwardly. She had always been a stickler for romance, and she often romanticized situations in her life because she found romance with men lacking. Perhaps Mary had been right, and if she was Maeve reincarnate, she had romanticized the whole terrible ordeal with Cotswold, to the point that her memories were completely skewed. Audrina snorted and rolled onto her side. How was she ever going to fall asleep without her pictures?

⚜

She was ready. Tonight, was the night. She pinned the tartan into place with the kilt pin he had given her as an early wedding gift. The castle was abuzz with a titillating excitement that was at the same time hushed and subdued. No one must know. She kept sneaking glances out the window in hopes of catching a glimpse of her Colin. It wasn't as if they hadn't spent every single waking moment of every single day together. He was there where she began, and she was his, where she started. They were the beginning, middle, and end of one another. The solid unit in a unified cord woven of love. There was no denying it, although she had tried time and time again. Colin's infuriating endless patience, never ceased to amaze her. But he had worn her down, until she secretly agreed to wed him in the middle of the night.

She felt they would be thick as thieves, stealing the rights of Prima Noctem away from the English. They planned to do it right under Lord Cotswold's nose, so that when he learned of their marriage, it would be too late for him to claim the right. Maeve had always felt the right had never been his to take anyway. It was between God, her and her Colin. But such was not the way with the laws of men. She never understood why the English couldn't just leave them in peace. It wasn't as if they were thrilled to be occupying the land anyway. They had neither the will nor the spirit to survive Scotia's harsh climates and seasons. But Maeve shook her head, clearing her thoughts of the vile Lord Cotswold. She'd observed him at a distance the few times he'd ridden into Claran Castle's courtyard to gloat over his reign of the area. He'd driven Uncle Dougal to the point of insane hatred, but there was little he could do about it.

Maeve spent the next few hours, wiling away the time until Mary would escort her down to the chapel in the middle of the night. The wedding party was small, consisting of Colin, herself, Mary, Alisdair, Donal and the priest. Mary felt sure no one would know of what they had done until after the ceremony took place, and Colin rushed her up here to the chamber to... well...she blushed thinking of the things they were going to do in that bed. She'd stayed true to her maidenhood, but it hadn't been for Colin's lack of trying to steal it from her.

When the door creaked open, and Mary ushered her to the door, she bounded down the steps behind her soon to be mother-in-law, giddy with excitement. They hastened to the back door which led through the gardens and out to the chapel. Mary squeezed her hand in as much excitement as she was feeling, and the two of them entered the back of the chapel. Maeve could practically hear her heart pumping it was beating so fast. Mary gave her a peck on the cheek, and Maeve waited at the back of the chapel anxiously, until Mary came back to escort her forward.

Alisdair met her in the dark, opting to give her away as the bride. She looked at him with sisterly affection, as they had often teased one another and jested about all manner of things. Alisdair had never been interested in her, he'd long ago had his eye on another, but he often confided in her about his secret love of the blacksmith's daughter, Rowena. Maeve had encouraged him to pursue her, but Alisdair was mighty in battle and wielding a sword, he was deadly shy when it came to matters of the heart.

He gave her a peck on the cheek and whispered, "Ye look radiant, sister."

She smiled up at him. "Thank ye, brother." And then Mary poked her head in the antechamber and ushered them forward.

Maeve's stomach fluttered with nerves as she approached the pulpit. Colin stood to the side of the priest who was new to the keep. He'd come from another clan when their priest had taken ill. Apparently, he had gotten well, and the young priest was sent on *his way, traveling to find a new clan to serve.*

Colin looked resplendent. He was dressed in his finest kilt and sporran. He had on a clean white linen shirt and his boots were polished. He wore his ceremonial claymore and Balmoral which were saved for dress occasions, and the smile he wore on his face when he saw her in the gown and clan colors, was none the likes that she had ever seen. She practically dragged Alisdair down the aisle in order to get to him.

When she arrived at the pulpit, she only had eyes for her Colin. She wondered why she had ever doubted him. She had been so foolish to wait. Colin took her hands in his and the priest bound them with a ceremonial cloth and spoke the words of the ceremony first in Gaelic and then in Latin as was custom.

When it was time to say the vows, Maeve breathlessly proclaimed, "I do."

And then in a loud clear voice, Colin said them back. There was no mistaking it. There were enough witnesses to their ceremony that they were well and truly wed.

Colin crushed her to him and kissed her like she was the very air he needed to breathe. Maeve felt the warmth grow in her belly that she always felt when she was wrapped in Colin's arms. She didn't want the kiss to end, but for proprieties sake, the priest cleared his throat and Colin broke the kiss off.

Mary and Alisdair congratulated them both, and little Donal ran to her and gave her a hug, telling her she was always the sister he had wanted and never had. They were the picture of a hail and happy family and Colin stopped to kiss her once more when the doors to the chapel burst open and the clanking of boots sounded on the stone floor.

Mary screamed and Alisdair shouted as he reached for his sword. In all the confusion, Maeve was unsure what was going on until she heard the unmistakable sound of horse hooves, sound in the chapel itself! She looked around and Colin's face was a sheet of white fury as Lord Cotswold rode his stallion into the chapel and confronted them both.

"So, you thought to wed in secrecy, did you?" He didn't wait for an answer.

"It is no matter, I have my ways of knowing what happens around here." And with that, he flung a bag of coins at the young priest who stooped to pick them up. He gave an almost apologetic look at Colin and Maeve as he hastened out the door. Alisdair lunged for him, but one of the soldiers drove the butt-end of his sword into his stomach, knocking the wind out of him.

Mary clung to Donal who was struggling in her grip to get away, but any ill-move toward the English could result in any one of their deaths. Lord Cotswold looked at Mary and tsked.

"I'd hold onto that child if I were you. He'll be a man in a decade or so and you wouldn't want to see him meet his maker upon the noose." Mary didn't say a word, but Cotswold continued. "It's a shame I hadn't been stationed in this God forsaken pit of a country, you might have provided an evening or two of entertainment, but I do like it when they're fresh." With that he turned from Mary dismissively, but not before he leered at her.

He turned to Colin and Maeve and said, "By the rights of the King, I claim this bride under the right of Prima Noctem. She will come with us now, so I may perform the husbandly duties that his Grace has seen fit to bestow upon the English Lordships."

"Please Lord Cotswold, doonae take her!" Colin pleaded. But his begging fell on deaf ears as Lord Cotswold rode up to them and began circling them on his horse.

"It is true, I find the Scottish brides to be, less, of a tousle in bed, however as Lord, it is not only my right, it is my duty to breed the barbaric traits of the Scots blood from the people. She comes with me now."

With that, he turned and began riding away. Maeve shrieked and clung to Colin who jumped at Lord Cotswold's leg, trying to claw him and rip him down off his horse. The soldiers with Lord Cotswold split in half. Half threw a sack over Maeve's head and carried her off, and the other half beat Colin to the floor until he was left lying there, broken and bleeding.

Maeve lost track of time as she was thrown over the back of a horse. She was mortified when she felt the pawing at her backside and heard the crude remarks the soldiers made to Lord Cotswold about her figure. More than once she felt them pinch at her breasts as they'd ride up beside whoever's horse she was on, and when the soldier who was carrying her tried to worm his fingers up her wedding dress, between her thighs, she bit his thigh through the fabric of the sack over her head.

He slapped her hard so that she felt black spots form over her eyes. Not that it would have made much difference, she couldn't see through the sack anyway, but she was humiliated as they paraded her through the streets with her dress hiked up to her hips while they all pinched and squeezed her buttocks, exposing her to God and everyone to see.

Maeve was numb with cold as they rode through the night to Cotswold Castle. She was numb in her mind as she had closed her emotions off to the soldiers and the attentions they were giving her on the ride.

She figured, if she didn't react and she didn't respond to them, they couldn't affect her, so she allowed herself to become lost in the memory of Colin and all the times they'd shared together. She prayed they had left him alive when they left. She decided to believe that he was, because the soldiers were laughing about how they had beaten him. But she didn't hear any tell of mortally harming him. She knew Mary would look after him until she could return. If she returned. Rumors had amassed and spread even to Claran Castle of Lord Cotswold's sadistic tendencies. It was rumored some brides never made it home to their newly wed husbands. Maeve was determined to make it home to her Colin, and she would close herself off from Cotswold, just as she had done with the soldiers.

When they arrived, she was flung from the horse and landed in what she suspected was horse dung. Men all around her laughed as she was dragged to her feet and forced to walk behind a soldier. He dragged her along by the binds of her hands which cut into her wrists, but he refused to take the blindfold off.

"Please, take the hood off so I can see where I am walking?" she implored.

He laughed as he said, "No, this will serve to remind you that save from the feel of the silk between your thighs, his Lordship doesn't wish to look upon your Scotch face any more than he has to. You're beneath him. Just a duty he must perform in the name of the crown. English women are far superior and easier on the eye than you swine!"

Maeve felt her cheeks burn under the hood. She'd never met a proper English lady, but she wondered if they really were better looking.

As they climbed the steps, the soldier tossed her into the room and she was finally rid of the hood. She was sweating and there was no water, but she managed to free herself of her binds. She passed the time before the evening, thinking of her Colin and praying he was alright, and when she felt the rush of Catriona and Moria's words as they entered her, "Remember that peace doth *dwell in Scotia's free, that sister's alike, raise magic from sea to sea. Her lands and her shores, fill witches with power that may be used in times of desperate hour."*

Maeve began the ritual of blessing the pin with the spell to send her in her reincarnate form and her pin back to her love. The spell wasn't a curse, but one forged of love and longing for the one she so desperately craved, and yet had been denied. She remembered her sister's wisdom that she must include the span of time and space, as her reincarnated form may not be of this time and place, so she worked the incantation so that it included both of those aspects.

"Bone of my bone, flesh of my flesh, through spans of time, I cannot rest. Seek thee my kin, and pardon my sin, that I may reincarnate, and new life begin. And with this pin I shall be returned to my love, cast through the ages, by touch of mine blood, and light from sun up above."

She hid the pin in the loose stone after that. Scotland's magic once again coming to her aid. As the castle was made of Scottish hewn stones, she willed the stone tower to show her the hiding place, and she prayed Lord Cotswold and his men wouldn't find it. Just as she stepped back from the hiding place, the footsteps could be heard on the steps and the door burst open.

Two soldiers rushed in and grabbed her by her arms. She struggled against their grip but went deadly still when a third came in, brandishing a knife that he then used to cut away her wedding dress. It fell to the floor in tatters and he then cut off her shift, so she was left standing naked and shivering as he ran the blade down the tip of her breast and leered at her as Lord Cotswold came in behind him.

"Now, now, you can have your fun with the Scottish bitch after I'm done with her and if there's anything left."

Maeve had promised to close herself off to him, but as he started toward her, she realized one thing, he was definitely going to hurt her, and he was certainly going to kill her, but she was not going to lie down docilely whilst he did. She kicked and clawed and scratched at any limb she could get near until they were forced to bind her. She continued to struggle after, not making it easy for him at all, but it was to no avail. Maeve screamed as the pain began, but was grateful for the blur of red that clouded her vision.

CHAPTER 19

Audrina woke with a start, sobbing hysterically. It took a moment for her sight to clear of the red blur she was seeing. When she was able to partially see again, she tried to sit up, but sort of rolled off the bed. She crawled to the window and pulled herself up by reaching up to the sill and grasping it. When she was in an upright position, she took great gulps of fresh air, as she tried not to be sick.

She remembered everything. Everything that was done to her, to Maeve. She knew now without a shadow of a doubt that she was the reincarnated Maeve. She felt everything Maeve had felt, and she felt. Every. Atrocious. Thing. Lord Cotswold had done to her. She sobbed anew at the memories. The acts of atrocity that he had committed in his sadistic pleasure hadn't been defined. It was the pain it had caused that Audrina remembered in vivid detail. Parts of her body throbbed in pain in a way that she was unaware could hurt as such.

What sickened her even more was the fact that, he hadn't been able to fulfill his "duty" as he proclaimed, unless he had been partaking of his sadistic nature. He was a sexual sadist and he reveled in the pain her caused, he got off on it.

Audrina continued to gasp as she willed her mind to turn to other thoughts. She was certain now of her love for Colin, and she clung to it as if it was the life saver she was so desperately clawing for. She was drowning in a sea of emotions and she needed her rock, her savoir and she knew without a doubt that had always been and always would be Colin.

She remembered the day she walked through the gates she was now staring at. She remembered the standoff with young Colin and at first, she had despised him for not accepting her straight away, but when he fell and cut his chin, all of that had fled from her soul as she realized, he was just like her, struggling to survive in a harsh and cruel world that showed no mercy to the sick and the weak. Maeve had decided right then and there that this boy was hers. God may have taken her family and her sisters from her in the epidemic, but he gave her back someone else, Colin.

Audrina remembered growing up in the keep and the day Colin had given her the tower room to practice her medicine. She had flounced around the room touching everything. He had worked the wood to create the benches and work tables for her and he had collected her stores from her room while she slept and organized them on the shelves. He had done it for her for her eighteenth birthday, a year before they would be parted from one another upon her death.

Audrina remembered why she had men's clothing in her trunks. Maeve and Colin would sneak out of the castle, just as Donal had done to ride his horse in the fen, and they would run into the woods and swim in the creek together on a hot summer's eve when the humid air was too much to combat with a wet cloth and a pat down upon their brows. Colin had taught her to swim in the creek and they would cool off with one another, and occasionally explore other aspects of their relationship if they were in the mind to do so, and they often were, resulting in having to cool off before they went too far, with another dip in the cool water.

They would then sneak back into the castle where Colin kept a spare change of clothes in her trunk, so he didn't risk waking Alisdair when they still shared a chamber with one another as young men.

After the death of Uncle Dougal, and before they were to be wed, Colin had moved into his old chamber, but they kept the spare clothes there, out of habit. Maeve would sometimes exchange her nightshift for his long linen shirt, because it felt as if she was being wrapped in one of his hugs.

Audrina felt the tears slipping down her cheeks as the memories came crashing back down around her. She knew she had been Maeve, and she knew Maeve was her. They were one soul sharing one body with the duality of two very different minds that were warring at the dynamic between the two, and anxiously seeking the reprieve of melding together to become one.

She understood the way the spell on the pin worked now. It hadn't been a curse after all. It had been a calling to Scotland's magic and mystery. The same feeling of kinship and longing she felt for the place she had never stepped foot on, was because she had stepped foot on it, in another lifetime. She recognized the words her sisters had told her about the way Scotia's magic worked. It was elemental in nature. Everything was one and the one made up everything. The very sun that beat down on Scotland's lands, was the same sun to beat down upon all the land, and in its light, find and recognize the blood of Maeve MacClaran and call her home. The blood was the key, when Audrina's blood spilt over the pin, and the sun shone on it, the elemental magic worked its will and brought her home. When she lost the pin in the bog, wherever it had fallen with her blood on it, once the sun shone on it, it transported itself to her and to where she belonged, in Colin's keep.

Audrina's mind began to swim as she missed her sisters. Her quest to find as much detail about her family with her grandfather, paled in comparison to finding the memories that had been locked away in her mind. She remembered Moria's sassy temperament and Catriona's firm resolve to teach Maeve, a young, six-year-old little girl as much magic as she could before the ravages of life and time staked their claim over her mortal self. Audrina was certain she would one day meet her sisters again, but in the now, she was still struggling to come to terms with herself.

What did all of this mean now that she had her memories back? It was as if a great veil had lifted itself and with clarity it also brooked uncertainty. Could she trust her own mind? Had her life in San Francisco been real? Her mind told her that essentially yes, it was. Her grandfather had still raised her, but also her Uncle Dougal had raised her. She had been a trauma nurse with a love of romance novels and pictures, but she also was a healer and endless pursuant of the dashing young Colin MacClaran.

Audrina felt as though the weight that had been lifted, also presented its own set of tangles and traps, ensnaring her in a web of questions and doubts. Would Colin recognize her as his true love if she tried to explain to him that she was the reincarnate of Maeve? Would he believe her that not only did she now hold all of Maeve's memories, thoughts and feelings, but she retained her own as well, as Audrina James? She had so many questions yet unanswered, and so many new truths to ponder, she didn't know who to turn for answers. She wondered if praying might help. Her grandfather always told her, when in doubt, give him a shout.

But would the Lord recognize her and answer her prayers? She was a witch after all and Audrina knew that especially in this age, witches and religion, did not mix. Sure, there were practicing Wiccans in her time, but they incorporated some of the Christian views into their own practices, some even professing their belief in God. They simply chose to believe in the magic of the universe as well. It largely coincided with how Audrina felt about the 'higher power', but how was she going to explain this all to a group of people who would more as like, burn her at the stake for merely mentioning the word witch, than accept her for who she was.

Audrina's head pounded, and she gazed into the star-filled night and wondered what she would do now. She glanced around the courtyard and espied the tiny chapel that was sitting at the far end. It looked barren and unused. She wondered if anyone went in there anymore, as she had yet to see any lights on inside the chapel and she had never heard of anyone mention a service.

Audrina decided if she was going to make peace with anyone, she would first need to make peace with God about all of this. She gathered her kilt that Colin had given her. It must have been an extra that Colin had made for Maeve as a wedding present. She had been wearing one when she was taken, and he had obviously kept this one wrapped for the past year and given it to her upon her return. She suspected he had several made, because until Maeve was wed into the MacClaran family, tradition dictated that she wore the James tartan, as it was still her kin. Audrina took comfort in recalling the finite details of Scottish customs that her grandfather had instilled upon her, and she wrapped them in her mind like a cloak, just as she wrapped the tartan around her body and secured it in place with the pin.

She carefully tiptoed to the door and listened to hear if anyone was outside in the hallway. When she opened the door, she was grateful someone had oiled the hinges, because it slid open silently. Audrina tiptoed down the hallway and descended the stairs. She recalled from memory that Mary had escorted Maeve to the chapel by the back door of the great hall and she too went out that door, as it deposited her next to the back door of the chapel.

Audrina looked left and then right and then stole across the courtyard until she reached the door to the antechamber of the chapel, and she carefully eased it open. Her heart was fluttering, but she was grateful that everyone was asleep at such a late hour and that she wouldn't be stopped and questioned for her presence in the chapel. She sat at one of the pews, praying quietly and thinking she was alone. She was alone in her mind, but what she did not see was Colin in a dark alcove of the chapel, watching her and listening to her prayers.

CHAPTER 20

"**G**od, if you can hear me, are you listening? I don't know what to do. The memories…they've come back to me now and I don't know if I should tell Colin and the others. What if they think I'm crazy or persecute me for being a witch? I don't want to lie, but I don't know what else to do," Audrina spoke quietly into the dark.

She looked around her and began to notice shapes in the dark. There were several worn wooden benches and the pulpit was plain and unadorned. Audrina saw simple wooden crosses lining the walls in between the windows. Everything was covered in a fine layer of dust, like the chapel hadn't been used in a while. She wondered if Colin had neglected it after such a sacrilegious and treacherous betrayal that the priest committed against he and Maeve. She was sure that must be the reason, but it saddened her that he had lost his faith. Like her, she was sure he still retained some of his faith, believing in a higher being, but he had his own issues to sort out with his relationship with God.

Audrina spoke again, "I would feel bad about lying, but what else should I do? Should I pretend I really did lose my memory? They already think it is so. Would one tiny lie outweigh the shadow of a larger one?" Again, her words rang out in the darkness and echoed off of the barren walls.

There was a peace to be found there, in the shadows of the night in the darkened chapel. It had once bore witness to a great tragedy, but Audrina found the peace lay in the simplicity of the tiny chapel. It was sure to have seen many marriages and Christenings, and even deaths. Audrina found the peace in this revelation, because at least one who passed and was sent to heaven within the walls of this chapel, would have found more peace than poor Maeve.

Audrina remembered the funeral for her grandfather like it was yesterday. It had been in a small parish, much like this one. He hadn't wanted anything large and flashy, but that was who he had been as a person. He was always quiet and reserved and with the exception of a few of his poker buddies, no one else except she and the priest had been in attendance that day. She listened to his words about ashes to ashes and dust to dust, and she pondered over them, wondering at the time if that meant he had become a part of something larger. Maybe that was the great power or being that people put their faith in. Would his ashes someday become part of the particles floating downriver in a stream that was bottled and shipped to third world countries to save the life of a child who was dying of thirst? Audrina hadn't understood these thoughts at the time, but with all of her revelations about Maeve, she was certain she somehow understood it better now.

Through Maeve's blood, her blood, she was able to come full circle and return to her Colin. She wasn't sure what that meant though, just that it was. Did that make her destiny as Maeve fulfilled? What did that mean for her, Audrina? Were the two inevitably and irrevocably interlocked and this was as it was meant to be from the start? Or had

Maeve's meddling with the magics and witchcraft been the catalyst that tied the two of them together?

Audrina rocked back and forth on the pew, humming an old hymn that her grandfather used to sing. She found it brought her comfort and solace in a time where she was mourning the death of her modern life and celebrating the rebirth of a life that had been taken all too soon.

Audrina wondered what had happened to poor Maeve? What had Cotswold done with her body? She was sure that Colin and his family had a burial practice they would have liked to have performed in her honor. Had they? Were they forced like some parents of missing children in the modern day, to officially declare her missing and deceased? Did they perform a ceremony, only to be left partially empty inside, knowing they would never know for certain if she was truly gone? Audrina mourned for them. She mourned for Maeve.

She couldn't bear to sit still any longer, so she got up and paced the chapel. It didn't take her long to come full circle and walk down the center aisle. Memories of euphoria and ecstatic gaiety filled her as she recounted Maeve's anticipation of meeting Colin down the center aisle. Audrina walked the very path that Maeve did and let herself come to rest in front of the pulpit. She turned to a non-existent Colin and said aloud the very words Maeve had on the day of her wedding. She felt a sense of serenity wash over her, like part of her soul that had not become raveled in Colin's was finally laid to rest, the frayed edges that Cotswold had snatched at, slowly unwinding her at her core, were now singed from Cotswold's grasp, and the cauterization could finally be laid to rest. She, Audrina, knew what had happened to Maeve. Maybe someday others would know too, but for now, it was enough that she knew.

None of this made her have any insights as to what to do about Colin and his family. Surely, they would want answers, or results someday. They would expect her to have a kinship with them over time. Of course, their unending patience and acceptance would have provided that anyway. They were good and honest people who loved, laughed, played, worked and worshiped and Audrina would have fallen for each and every one of them in her own way. But what they sought from her, she was unsure she knew how to give.

Audrina approached the pulpit and rounded the small stand. She glanced down at the passage that lay open in the bible. It was the same passage the priest had read from when Maeve and Colin had been wed, thus confirming Audrina's suspicions that no one had used the chapel since that dreadful night.

Audrina read aloud, *"1 Corinthians 13:4-5: 'Love is patient, love is kind. It does not envy, it does not boast, it is not proud. It does not dishonor others, it is not self-seeking, it is not easily angered, it keeps no record of wrongs'."*

She thought about this passage. Colin, her love certainly had been patient. Would he continue to be patient with her if she chose not to tell him? He had also been exceedingly kind. As had Mary and Alisdair. Even little Donal had taken her in, without so much as a fuss. They must have loved Maeve fiercely for them to be so passionate about a virtual stranger. But again, Audrina's consciousness warred with her, wondering if they would turn on her if she told them the truth. Audrina re-read the passage. Would lying to them constitute dishonoring them? If Colin found out the truth, would he think less of her for having known only Cotswold? It would definitely be self-serving of her to reveal nothing to anyone, and it was sure to incite anger in her family should they find out she was lying to them.

Audrina sighed and gingerly closed the bible. A cloud of dust poofed up from the pages when the book slammed shut. She still had no idea what to do in regard to Colin and his family. If the verse was to be believed, then they would not keep record of her transgressions, but Audrina's problem was, she now had the memories and actions of two lives to keep record of.

"Are we not our own harshest judge, juror and executioner?" Audrina shook her fist at the cross. "Send me a sign! Tell me what to do!" she cried. Her world was so chaotic, and the old adage was 'the Lord works in mysterious ways.' The problem for Audrina was, thus far the mystery only continued to deepen, with no end in sight as to any revelations for her, or Maeve.

Audrina dusted her hands off on her lap and walked back toward the antechamber of the chapel. She was no closer to finding answers here than she was in her chamber, and she figured she had best hurry back there, before her presence was missed.

As she passed through the antechamber, she saw a shelf of books which held journals. With her curiosity piqued, she walked over to the shelf and pulled one of the journals down from the shelf. She flipped it open the last entry, and noted the date, for one-year prior, and the name of the priest, Father Gavin Graham. She could barely make out the words, but his inscription was to note the marriage of Colin MacClaran to Maeve James. He'd signed and dated the entry, and Audrina ran her finger over the faded ink. She suddenly got a flash of the thief that had tried to steal the kilt pin that day at the museum. Was it possible that like her ancestry, Father Graham, a scoundrel of a man had also passed down a legacy? What if he had been so adamant that "thou shall not suffer a witch to live" was his reasoning for betraying Maeve and Colin. What if he too passed down to his kin, the same zealous religious views, and generations of Grahams related to the Father had been searching for the pin, so that Maeve could never be reincarnated from the dead? Cotswold surely had a hand in the priest's treachery, but what if that was only fueled by a burning hatred that was already emblazoned within the priest's heart? Rumors had already spread that Maeve practiced witchcraft. Her healing capabilities alone were testament to that. What if the rumors were fueled by the reputation of her sisters and then compounded by the unholy light that blazed high in that tower that night?

With more questions than answers, Audrina

snapped the book shut and put it back on the shelf. She didn't see anyone sneak back to the castle ahead of her, which was why she was surprised when she found Colin waiting for her at her chamber door.

CHAPTER 21

"Colin!" Audrina cried. "What are you doing here?"

"I could say the same tae ye, lass," he said softly looking around. "Now, are ye goin' tae let me in so we can discuss what I just heard ye confess in the chapel?"

Audrina's blood ran cold. She had confessed, out loud that she had her memories back. What was she going to tell him? Everything was still a bit of a blur. Her memories were there, but they were unfocused, like they were trying to mesh with the ones from her modern life.

"Oh, very well, come in," she snapped. She felt trapped, but she certainly wasn't going to have this conversation out in the hall where anyone could hear them.

Audrina immediately went to the window and looked down at the chapel. She had been foolish not to double check that no one was following her. What was she going to say to him?

"Lass…" Colin began.

She placed her hands on the window sill and held on firmly. She refused to turn around and look at him because then he might see the truth in her eyes.

"Lass, look at me," he pleaded with her.

Audrina sucked in a breath and shook her head. There was no way she could face him. She wasn't prepared for this, and she knew she would quail under the heat of his gaze and confess all and she wasn't ready for that. How dare he listen in on such a private confession? It was with this heated thought that she spun on her heel before she realized what she was doing. She opened her mouth to tell him off, but he cut her off.

"I heard ye confess. Ye told the Lord above ye have yer memories back. Tell me, what happened tae ye, Maeve."

Audrina shut her mouth. He still believed she was just Maeve and that she hadn't died, but been kept prisoner this past year, and was just now returning to him. Audrina wracked her brain for something to say.

"I told you the truth the first time," she blurted before she could really think about what she was saying.

"Lass…" he spoke to her like he was trying to reason with an unruly child.

"No! Colin! I'm not a child! Don't speak to me as such! I told you, I woke up in that field and I traveled to the town and saved Donal and that's the truth of it! Why won't anyone believe me!" she cried. She paced back and forth in front of the window, flustered and agitated.

"I do believe ye," he said simply.

It made her stop pacing and look at him. She had blurted the simplest truth that she could think of, because she assumed that like the simplicity of the chapel, there was something honest and true about it. It somehow made it, humble. Now Colin was standing there telling her he believed her. The frustration that stemmed from that was, she didn't know what to do with that.

"So where does that leave us, Colin? Answer me that? What the bloody hell are we supposed to do now?" she yelled. She was so frustrated and the only person she had been able to take her inner turmoil, fear and anger out on was herself. It was easy shouting at Colin, he just stood there and took it. If he was angry about it, he didn't show it, and yet, somehow that unending patience he had for her was even more enraging. "Why are you just standing there?" she shouted.

Her life had become a mess and she was tired of being the only one to wallow in it. She wanted someone else to feel as miserable as she did the last few days and as confused and chaotic as she did, and she charged on ahead with her temper, in an attempt to bring Colin along with her.

"What the bloody hell do ye want me tae say, Maeve? That I heard it all? That I ken ye've got yer memories back, whate'er they may be, but I cannae help ye cope w'it them until ye confide in me? We were married remember? We're supposed tae sort these things out together. The madness and all that. But ye willnae let me in. Ye've closed yerself off tae me and I doonae ken how tae reach ye and ye willnae e'en let me bloody try!" he thundered back at her.

Audrina felt the tears prick the back of her eyes. He was a man standing there telling her something, but she didn't know what. What she did know was it was important.

"What do you want from me, Colin? Do you want me to be Maeve? Is that it? Do you want me to lie to you and tell you what you want to hear so that things can go about being normal or whatever that is around here?" Audrina realized she had marched up to him and was standing nose to nose with him. Both of them were breathing hard and their concentration was only broken by the shuffling outside the door. Apparently, they had woken people up, and the people were debating whether they should come in and intercede or not.

Audrina glanced at the door and then flipped her braid over her shoulder, bit her lip and blew out a frustrated breath. She realized at the same time that Colin smiled down at her, that it was a gesture that Maeve used to do all the time. Colin used to tease her so that he would cause that very reaction.

When next he spoke, his words were soft, and kind and they completely took her by surprise. "What I want from you lass, Maeve, Audrina, whate'er ye wish tae call yerself, it doesnae matter tae me, because what I want from ye, is tae be happy. And if that means ye believe yer memories are tellin' ye that ye were deeply hurt by Cotswold, and ye cannae think o'another way tae deal w'it them other than believin' in yer life ye've created in

San Francisco; and aye, I believe one way or another, ye've created that life, whether the truth o'it is real tae me or not, it's real tae ye, or ye fell through the bloody sands o'time because ye died and God Himself brought ye back tae me, whate'er ye believe, I want it tae make ye happy. I'll take it. I'll wait, lass. I've been waitin' for ye me whole life and I'll continue tae wait for ye tae come back tae me."

Audrina gasped as he placed a gentle kiss on her forehead and turned and walked out the door. She watched his retreating back as he yielded the battle field to her, leaving it her decision to go to him or not. She was certain he would not bow down so quietly, save for tonight for her peace of mind, but he was proving to her that he would wait as long as it took for her to come back to him.

Audrina sat on her bed a long time before she finally laid down and tried to sleep. She wasn't sure what triggered in her mind first, the fact that she wasn't sleeping, or the fact that she wasn't sleeping because she was caught up in taking in all the details of the drawings that had been fastened to the ceiling above her bed. At first, she didn't know what they were, then she realized as she stared up at them, she was staring at pictures of a large bridge, a huge tree that resembled a sequoia, and pictures of her childhood home as she had described them to Colin yesterday as she lay in his arms describing all these things to him.

He had used his imagination, and clearly his artistic skills to replicate what she had described using only her words. Of course, the bridge was off, a medieval Scotsman wouldn't have any concept of how massive the Golden Gate Bridge really was, but the design was there. She saw a small woman at the base of the sequoia tree and it dawned on her that he had tried to sketch her, or Maeve at the base of the tree. Perhaps he had done this for his own bene-fit, to understand the vastness of the trees that she had been talking about. And then she thought perhaps he really did understand the wide expanse and magnitude of nature, being a native from the highlands of Scotland.

The last picture was her favorite. It was the little ranch house she and her grandfather had lived in before he passed. She had sold it when he died and moved into an apartment that was rent controlled and had all the modern amenities such as trash removal, a community pool, a maintenance line to call whenever she needed someone to look at the plumbing. She realized, she had purposefully isolated herself from what she held dear, a home with fine memories of a family, because she had been so confused, caught between two-time periods, and she didn't know where she fit anymore. She missed that house and Colin had done a remarkable job capturing its likeness. He had sketched the shutters to perfection. He had to ask what they were, as the castle didn't really have shutters like modern houses. He had sketched the little shrub gardens at the base of the front windows and the path that led to the front porch. He had sketched an old man in a rocker that, although looked nothing like her grandfather, the sentiment was there so it made the man in the picture all the more real to her.

Audrina knew they were Colin's drawings. Because he had signed them at the bottom where artists do. She had never anticipated that he partook of the arts, or anything of refinery, as his attentions were mostly spent in Lording over his people. She wasn't sure when they had been hung up. Perhaps before she had the last nightmare, and she just didn't notice them. Or perhaps when she went to wander down to the chapel, it didn't matter. All that mattered was, in these three drawings, Colin had proved just how much he loved her and cared for her. Even if that meant to him, entertaining her fantasy of another time and another life. Audrina made the second vow she had ever made to herself. She vowed that no matter how confusing life became with the knowledge of two souls living in it, she vowed she wouldn't shut Colin out of it, because he loved her no matter who she was.

CHAPTER 22

"Colin! You can't catch me, Colin!" Maeve called. A great splash sounded and then she shrieked as she tried to swim away. The problem was, she wasn't sure where he had gone. He was always showing off, proving to her that he could swim underwater. She hadn't been able to do that yet. He had just started to teach her to swim, and he teased her about being a witch. He told her he was secretly testing her in the trial by water. It was an ancient test that determined if the person was a witch, based on whether they survived being thrown in a rushing body of water. Maeve was certain the only rushing of the creek, was during the spring thaw. The *majority of the time, it trickled by the keep idly and with tiny splashes and visible trout swimming along lazily in the sun.*

Colin had found a pool that the creek gathered in as it ran its way south, and it had flooded the inlet that rested past some rocks, before a small waterfall sent it cascading further down until it ran itself into another trickling stream. It was in the pool that they found solace from the hot summer sun. They had snuck out of the keep through the back door by the chapel again. Maeve had worn her nightshift, and her undergarments, a small pair of pantaloons and a chemise. She would swim in the undergarments and wear the night-gown home to climb into bed. Then by the time the sun rose the next day, the undergarments would be dried.

Maeve looked around in the black water, unable to see anything, because they never dared risk taking a torch with them, lest they were discovered. What would people say to see her in such a state of undress, with the Laird's nephew of all people? He always opted to swim in naught but his trews, a state of undress that still made her blush, but they had grown up together, so it wasn't as if she hadn't seen it all before. Actually, it had been a few years since she had seen it all. Around the time his voice deepened, and her chemise began to fill out. But they had remained fast friends, not letting their budding bodies deter them from their closeness.

This was a game Colin liked to play. He'd swim underwater, so she would lose track of him, and then as she stared around, looking for shadows in the moonlight cast upon the water, he would break the surface of the water, and grab her ankles. She would shriek and splash at him, and then they would scooch down and wait and listen to see if anyone heard her shrieks of fright and come running.

Tonight, had been no different. Colin had scared her twice now already, and she had threatened to cut him down when he was sleeping with his claymore, but he had tugged at her braid and swam away. She had been remiss to leave the pool, because the night had been so humid, and her room was stifling hot, as the last rays of the sun always beat down upon her chamber window. She had slipped the small parchment of paper under Colin's door, there nightly signal for if they were to go swimming or not. She never drew anything more than the symbol of waves on the parchment, or the symbol with an x through it. This was to keep anyone from discovering their rendezvous. Sometimes Mary would come in and work on her embroidery with Maeve, and on those nights of womanly gossip, she was unable to get away.

Maeve had slipped him the parchment tonight, and they had met in the grove of rowan trees, before making the trek to the pool. She wasn't sure why tonight had felt different, but perhaps it was the draw of the full moon. She was restless somehow, like she yearned for something she didn't understand. That's when she felt the pull of heat in her belly they seemed to be strung down to the apex of her thighs. The coil lay burning, hot and wet as she watched him disrobe to his trousers. She had turned away when he looked back at her, and she was unsure if he had caught her staring at him, but he said nothing when next his head crested the water in the middle of the pool.

She had cautiously waded into the pool, letting the coolness of the water wash over her skin and cool her down from the inside out. They had been swimming for what felt like the better part of the night now, and she was just ready to tell him they should get back, before they were discovered, when Colin had pulled his disappearing game.

She knew the contact was coming. She burned for the touch of his palm on her calf before it even happened. She was never going to tell him such a thing though. But when it came this time, she didn't jump and shriek shrilly, and she possibly should have, because the inaction, was as much of a tell as the act itself.

When Colin's head crested the water, he didn't move away as quickly, to avoid being splashed in the face with water. This was her typical reaction to his games, and when it didn't happen, he questioned her.

"Are ye alright, Maeve?"

"Och, aye," she responded and tried to turn away.

"Do I no' frighten ye anymore?" he asked softly. He was much too close and she felt her pulse race and her heart pound. It was same the same effect could be felt in such a different manner than fear.

"Nay, ye frightened me just fine, Colin. Tis just tha' I was expectin' it this time."

"Aye? And were ye expectin' me tae do this?" he asked just as his arm circled around her waist and pulled her to him. Before she could protest, he leaned down and kissed her. The kiss was soft and gentle at first, but the more she leaned into him, inviting him in, the more he deepened the kiss to a protective, claiming kiss. She'd wanted him to kiss her for years, but she'd never dared asked for it. Now, here he was, kissing her like he couldn't live without her kiss.

Maeve moaned as his hands began to roam the length of her back. He tugged gently at her braid, causing her to smile against his lips. His hands cupped her bottom through her pantaloons, the thin *fabric was already clinging to her skin from swimming. She gasped as he gave her bottom a squeeze, pulling, lifting and prying her apart. It caused her to press against him, and for the first time she allowed her fingers to intertwine with the blond curls on his chest and she ran her palms over the hard muscles of his abdomen. She felt the hard length of him pressed against her through their clothes, and she mewled into his mouth as he shifted his hips, so that it rubbed at her, causing a delicious friction.*

Maeve broke the kiss off as Colin's hand circled her waist and came up to cup her breast. His fingers wove in between the laces of her chemise and he pulled them free, baring her taught nipple to the moonlight. Maeve watched as his head bent and he sucked it into his warm mouth, and she felt the pull of his tongue as he teased the tight bud. His other hand went between them as he cupped her mound through her pants and she shuddered as he rubbed his palm against her, allowing her the pressure she discovered she desperately needed.

Maeve in turn let her hands wander

down over his stomach as he explored her other breast, and she palmed the length of him through his trews.

"Bloody hell, lass!" he croaked.

His voice was raw and needy and when she looked him in the face, he was panting, and his face was strained. She thought maybe she had hurt him, but then she recalled the time she and Colin had espied the thing Maudie did with her mouth to one of the men down at the pub in the back alley. He had the same look upon his face, but when it was over, he thanked Maudie again and again. She and Colin had laughed about it then, but she understood now that the pleasures of the flesh, transcended anything that made any sense to the rational human mind.

She squeezed and rubbed him through his pants, and she watched the different emotions that flickered over his face. He in turn, rubbed her continuously, focusing the butt of his palm on massaging the hard nub in the center of her folds. Whenever she felt more pressure there, the intensity of the feel-

ings grew until she couldn't stand it anymore.

"Colin!" she moaned. "Don't stop! That feels so good!"

He seemed to know what she needed, because just as she felt the pulse rip from her veins, he clutched her to him as her cries rang out through the night and she fell off the precipice of bliss. He held her and let her drift down onto his lap in the cool water, where she lay shivering in his arms. Colin, if he needed relief for himself, said nothing, but crooned to her in the mother tongue and she let the whisper of his Gaelic wash over her, just as the waves of pleasure had.

❦

AUDRINA AWOKE AND GROANED. SHE HAD FALLEN asleep at some point, looking at her new pictures. Colin had made her feel so at home by bringing home to her, that her mind finally had the opportunity to relax, and her memories had started sorting themselves out. Apparently, starting with some of her fondest memories of Colin when she had been Maeve.

Audrina threw her arm over her eyes, the heat of embarrassment reddening her cheeks. She looked then at her window, and realized the sun was up, and the early morning light told her if she didn't get down to breakfast, she was going to miss it, and she was hungry.

Audrina made her way down to the table. Thankfully, whether it was at the behest of Colin or not, they didn't say one word about her midnight sojourn to the chapel, or the argument she and Colin had gotten into. They all greeted her a good morning, and she gratefully settled into her seat next to Colin, who smiled at her, and offered her a tray of breads.

Audrina accepted, unable to bring herself to look at him, as the color in her cheeks had yet to dissipate, and she ate her bread in silent mortification.

"Lass, I ken ye didnae get tae bed until the hour was late, but did ye no' sleep well? Yer as flushed as a wee young sow."

Audrina choked on her bread, guessing he just told her she was as pink as a young piglet and she tried to think of something to say to him, but before she could he leaned in and whispered, "Or mayhap, lass, t'was tha' dream o' yers tha' has ye blushin' like a fair maiden. Did I no' hear ye moanin' in yer sleep last night? Somat aboot, Colin, tis so good. Please, doonae stop!"

Audrina hid her burning face behind her goblet of water and stared fixedly at her plate so that she wouldn't have to look him in the eye, and have him see the truth of how badly she wanted him.

CHAPTER 23

The next few days passed for Audrina in a peaceable calm that she hadn't felt in several days. Life amongst the people of Claran Castle was becoming one that Audrina found she could tolerate despite the lack of modern amenities. Audrina felt her every step dogged by Colin, but she began to understand that she didn't mind. Her fondness for his amicable conversations and friendly gestures were growing on her.

Two days passed since the embarrassing conversation at the breakfast table, and Audrina had been going to the tower at the back of the great hall and working on small poultices for her patients. Her aptitude for modern medicine had her weeding out any impractical treatments and categorizing the rest. Her first patient was Donal, who came to her with a scraped knee.

Audrina peeled back the dirty bandage he had wrapped around the scrape and asked, "How did you manage this injury?"

He grinned at her, but said nothing, indicating that he had been doing something youthfully nefarious, so she didn't press him any further. She cleaned and rebandaged the wound, but not before she applied a salve to help keep it from becoming infected. Donal had a bad habit of scampering away from the maids when they would bring his bath water to his chamber, and Audrina was worried he would go as many days as he could before practically being hogtied and thrown into the tub by Mary.

Mary also climbed the steps to the tower and they spent a lovely afternoon going over the various medicinal uses of some of the herbs that Audrina had dried up there.

"I suffer from bouts o'pain tae me forehead. I wasnae aware so many of these plants could help tae cure it," she told Audrina.

Audrina was grateful for the company, but in some ways, she wished Mary would go for her afternoon nap, because she had been spying on Colin who was working in the courtyard with his men. He had glanced up on occasion and she had ducked from the window.

It wasn't until the sun began to set that she heard footsteps on the stairs, she assumed Mary had sent another patient up to her, but when she turned around she found Colin standing in the doorway.

He looked around, as if he was trying to think of something to say, and Audrina waited. She hadn't asked permission to be up here, despite it being Maeve's, *her* tower to begin with.

"I thought ye might still be up here," he said quietly.

"Ahh, yes. I gave your mother something for her headache and made sure Donal's scraped knee doesn't become gangrenous."

"Gangrenous?" he reiterated.

"Umm, rotten. The imp doesn't bathe as regularly as he should. Aine was telling me the other day she had to chase him across the fen to get back to his chamber before the water ran cold."

"So ye've made some friends here then?" he asked quietly. He walked further into the room and sat down at the bench she had set near the work table.

"Yes, Aine is sweet. She's one of the maids who brings me my bath every night," Audrina replied.

"Aye, I ken who she is, she's me Da's cousin's wee lass."

"That's right, most everyone in Castle Claran would be related somehow," she said.

"Ye're likin' life here, at the Castle then?" he pressed a little more.

Audrina thought about it. She had made more friends here in only a few days than she had her entire life living in San Francisco. Would she really miss her life in the modern world? She had gained so much more that was worthwhile as she lived out her days in Castle Claran, 'allowing' her memories to slowly come back to her. The inhabitants of the keep didn't seem to mind that she picked up where Maeve had left off, as her duty as healer. Even Mary seemed ecstatic to be rid of some of the responsibility of running the keep. Aine had approached her yesterday and asked if she fancied water fowl or a pork roast for dinner, citing that Mary was in a fitful state with her headache and resting so she should go and ask her.

Audrina had sent word to Mary to come see her for the headaches the next day, and she had thanked her for carrying out the lady of the house duties the day prior. Audrina thought another moment as she ground some herbs into a paste of fat. It was smelly, but with a sprinkle of lavender, she could turn the salve into something resembling a burn salve for sunburns.

She thought about how happy she had been the last few days and she thought about how every time she caught sight of Colin, her heart did a little pitter patter dance in her chest and her stomach fluttered with butterflies. She liked it here, she was content.

"Yes, I am enjoying life here at the castle," she answered him honestly.

"Good, tis good," he replied.

"I never thanked you for my pictures," she murmured as she continued to work. She hadn't mentioned them the morning after she discovered them, because he had teased her so mercilessly about moaning in her sleep. She figured it was safe to bring them up now.

"I'm glad ye like them, lass, I thought it might help ye sleep at night," he responded.

Before she could stop herself, she blurted, "Why do you sleep outside my bedroom door? Why don't you go sleep in your room? It would be more comfortable for you."

"Because lass, ye might need me." His answer was simple enough, but Audrina still didn't fully understand.

"If I need you, I will come and find you."

"Aye, I ken ye will. But, tis also tha' yer in my room." He looked pensive.

"Oh, I'm sorry. Do you want me to move then?" she asked.

"Och, nay! Tha's no' what I meant at all. Tis just that we're married. And so, strictly speakin' yer in the bed I should be sharin' w'it ye." His eyes were full of mirth as the color rose in her cheeks.

"Oh. Well…" she trailed off.

"I'm no' goin' tae sneak into yer bed in the wee hours o' the mornin', lass. No' if ye don't want me there. T'was but a jest. I like tae see yer cheeks turn tha' rosy hue," he teased her.

Audrina clapped her palms over her cheeks and glared at him.

"Was there something you needed, Colin MacClaran?" she demanded, pretending to be annoyed with him so as to hide her embarrassment.

"Aye!" he said happily. A little too happily.

She wondered what his game was.

"I've a pain and a twitch in me arm."

She raised her eyebrows at him, but the look in

his eyes challenged her. She wiped her hands on a cloth and walked over to him.

"Which arm?" she demanded.

"This one." He held up his left arm.

"Yeah? Where?"

"Here." He pointed to a spot on his shoulder and she began prodding at it a little. She wasn't sure he had been telling the truth, but she continued to feel around for anything unusual.

"When did it start to hurt?" she asked, her brow furrowed as she concentrated.

"A few days ago," he murmured. He was so close, she could almost lean over and kiss him if she wanted to.

"And why didn't you tell anyone about it?" she asked.

"Because, there was no one tae tell a'the time."

"Does it hurt when I apply pressure to it?" she inquired.

"Nay, it travels up me arm here." He indicated a path along his shoulder with his right hand and placed it over his left pectoral.

Colin had been wearing nothing but his kilt with no linen shirt or pants because the summer sun was so hot. His chest was bared to her and she noted the fine curls of silver blond hair that were sprinkled over his muscles. The heady scent of his masculinity made her drowsy with desire, but she bit her lip in concentration as she placed her palm over his muscle.

"And why do you think it travels to this muscle?" she asked. She had never heard of such a pain. She would be concerned of a heart attack, but he was so young at only twenty-nine.

"Because, I've missed ye, lass." He looked deep in her eyes and her breath caught. He looked so sincere when he said it that Audrina felt tears form in the backs of her eyes.

"I…" she started, but before she could say another word, Colin leaned in and gave her the lightest brush of his lips across hers.

The act made her lips tremble and she was stunned into silence. He was so sweet and it made her crush on him grow every day. He didn't press for more, but got up quietly and walked out the door.

Audrina sat on the stool and pressed her fingers to her lips, as if she was rubbing her lips in an attempt to rub the kiss in and be burned onto her lips forever. No, life wasn't bad at Castle Claran, she realized. There were finally people in her life who loved and cared about her and missed her when she was gone. She hadn't had that since her grandfather had passed.

Audrina made her way downstairs a while later, just in time for dinner. Colin didn't say anything about the kiss, but when she sat down to eat, Alisdair scooted over to her and raised an eyebrow.

"Lass, we need tae talk." He was deadly serious.

"Alright, about what?" she asked. She was suddenly nervous, she had wondered if she had done something terribly wrong.

"Tis aboot tha' bloody beast o'yers," he growled.

"My beast?" She looked at Colin and a few of the men at the other tables let out a laugh. A cry went up about Colin slightly resembling a mad and hairy beast, and he responded something to them in Gaelic which made the women at the tables gasp. Audrina could guess at what he had said, but she turned her attention back to Alisdair.

"What beast?" she asked.

"The bloody coo," he retorted. He said 'bloody coo' like the animal was the devil itself reincarnate.

"The cow?" she asked.

"Aye, tis as ornery as an old wench. It willnae go out tae pasture w'it the rest o'the coos. I think ye've placed a spell o'er it and ye need tae go and encourage the wee devil, a'fore she kicks me shins again!" he thundered.

It took Audrina a moment to process what cow he was talking about, and why it was being ornery. Then she did something she hadn't done in days. She laughed so hard at the adamant expression on Alisdair's face, that she had tears running down her cheeks.

CHAPTER 24

After dinner the previous evening, Audrina was convinced half the castle thought she was mad, but she didn't care. Some claimed she had been having a fit of some kind, she was laughing that hard. Alisdair had threatened to slaughter the cow for steaks if she didn't try to woo the beast out of its stall, so Audrina had promised to go early in the morning when the rest were let out and see if she could convince the cow to move.

Audrina had always loved highland cows. She had seen a few at a fair she and her grandfather attended, and she was more content to stand near the stall and pet them, as they were docile creatures, than she was to play any of the expensive games or ride on the flashy rides. She was six at the time and had tried to convince her grandfather to buy her one as a pet. He'd asked where she planned to keep it and she had told him without hesitation that it could sleep on the front porch.

She never got her pet cow, but she did get a stuffed highland cow that Christmas that she named Shamus.

Audrina rubbed at her sleepy eyes when she woke up. She smiled at her pictures on the ceiling and was delighted to find another sketch of her Bessie that had been slipped under the door sometime during the night. She would have to remember to ask Colin how he secured them to the ceiling for her, so she could add it to her collection that night.

Audrina quietly let herself out of her chambers, and true to his word, she carefully stepped over the sleeping figure of Colin. Someone had taken pity on him and brought a blanket that he had wadded up as a pillow, and he'd used his kilt as a blanket. She also made a note to herself to work harder at convincing him to find a spare bed. Or he could have her bed and she would go find a spare bed.

Audrina tiptoed downstairs and heard the muffled whisperings of some of the early risers in the castle, and she crept down the stairs and out the door. Once she was outside, she pulled her tartan around her shoulders a little tighter, so she could ward off the chill, and she let herself into the stables at the far end of the courtyard, past the chapel. The stables held rows and rows of stalls, and the early morning air was thick with puffs of breath from the dormant beasts. She began making her way down the rows so that she could spot the one with the white patch. She found her, in the very last stall on the left, and the greeting she received was just as jovial as the last two times she'd encountered her.

"Good morning," Audrina said as she gave her a scratch on the head. She leaned back as Bessie mooed and swung her head around, moving out of the way of her horns. Bessie snorted at her and nuzzled her palm, which she had the foresight to bring a treat with her. "Now, you get this only if you promise to go with the others." Audrina held it away from Bessie who looked at her from under the curtain of shaggy fur balefully. She held out the apple and Bessie slobbered on her palm and ate it up. She gave her another scratch and was about to turn and leave when Alisdair walked up beside her.

"Ye ken that's all it will take?"

"I honestly don't know," Audrina replied. "Good morning, by the way."

"Mornin', lass." He yawned and unhooked the

rope across the stall. He grabbed Bessie's lead line, and sure enough, she walked out into the hallway with him. "Ye always did ha' a way w'it them, Maeve." Alisdair looked at her thoughtfully. "Ye'd spend hours in here w'it them. Talkin and singin' tae them. We all thought ye were daft, but they brought ye peace somehow. Do ye remember?" he asked.

Audrina thought about it, and sure enough, the memories came swimming up in her mind, from Maeve's memories. Her sister Catriona had told her that all witches had a connection with the earth and with animals. Audrina recognized this for the lore that all witches have familiars. An animal that was her spirit animal. It struck Audrina funny that hers was a cow, but in some religions, cows were revered.

"Yes, I remember." She smiled at him and Bessie who mooed again.

"Mayhap tha's why ye cannae eat meat," he wondered out loud.

"Yes, perhaps," she concurred.

After she and Alisdair walked the cows to the pasture, they returned just in time for breakfast.

Audrina sat down next to Colin who wished her a good morning, and she just began digging into her food, when the doors to the great hall were thrown open. A hush fell over the dining crowd, and Audrina had a hard time seeing who was approaching. Colin went rigid beside her when he spotted him and gripped her arm.

"Colin, what is it?" she asked.

"Quiet, lass," he whispered to her.

Audrina continued to search the crowd, but heard his voice before she saw him. The familiarity sent a chill racing down her spine.

"Still making up for your lack of wife by stuffing your face I see, MacClaran." The voice was taunting and preceded by a feathery plumed hat that Audrina caught a glimpse of over the tops of the crowd. The entire hall was silent except the occasional crunch of some bit of food or that, as Lord Cotswold strode up the pathways that lead to the main table. He'd pause, occasionally taking a bite out of someone's food, and then spit it on the floor in disgust. "Not that anything on your tables is edible," the taunting voice called.

Audrina could feel Colin's hand slide between them to wear his sword lay sheathed. She saw soldiers march in and around all of the tables, their swords drawn and their uniformed figures standing at attention.

"Yes, I suppose you wouldn't have taken another

wife, not after the last one ran off and left you. That, and judging by the pickings you have available here, you'd be better off marrying the ass-end of a swine." Lord Cotswold finally came into view. He still wasn't looking at the head table, he was leering at all of the women around the great hall. His eyes fell on Mary first, and he quickly glanced away.

Audrina's blood ran cold when she saw him seek out Aine. Aine was just a slip of a girl at only fifteen, but she was beginning to show the budding signs of womanhood, and Cotswold clearly noticed too. He paused, leering at her, and a look of pure, raw lust came over his face, followed by a mask of passivity, but his eyes, his eyes were just as cold, sadistic and calculating. He must be wondering if she had any suitors yet. She was around the age for marrying, and Audrina feared he had just singled out his next victim.

Her stomach turned sour as she watched him look at Aine in such a way. Her vision clouded over in the red haze of her nightmare, as she came face to face with her murderer for the first time. Audrina couldn't breathe from the torrent of emotions that swept through her. Rage, anger, fear, hatred and revulsion washed over her in a tsunami effect. But the one feeling that Audrina clings to, that was her saving grace in the storm brewing within her, was the revenge she wanted. She had never felt anything so powerful in all her life. She wanted it more than anything she had ever wanted, save for Colin. The need to lash out and attack Cotswold was so intense, she had to grip the edges of her chair, to prevent herself from rising up and lunging at him.

Just as Audrina was willing herself to take a few, steadying breaths so that she wouldn't get them all killed, Cotswold turned to her and Colin, and for the first time, came face to face with her. His pale, watery blue eyes widened in horror. His portly body began to shake, causing the paunch of his belly to jiggle in his ridiculously overdressed pant and shirt suit. His pouchy face broke out into sweat and his curly iron gray hair which give away his aging form, plaster to his face. The suit was purple silk with gold trim and began to stain as he sweat in fear. The hat on top of his head matched the suit in color.

Cotswold's face paled as he lifted a silken gloved finger and pointed at her. "It cannot be!" he whispered. He took a step back as Colin stood up, placing a hand over her to shield her from his sight. But it was folly, Cotswold continued to back away, as his soldiers brandish their swords in obvious confusion.

"It cannot be!" Cotswold shouted again as his eyes locked onto Audrina. He took in her simple dress, and the clan tartan that she had worn since arriving here. It was the same dress that Maeve used to don, and with her red hair and brown eyes, he was staring at the doppelgänger of Maeve, not knowing she was really Audrina, but believing he was seeing the woman he murdered.

Cotswold turned on his silken, slippered feet, and to call his dash out the door a run would be assessing his gait slightly off kilter, but as he sprinted down the corridors, Audrina watched, half raised from her chair in an attempt to chase after the man that murdered her. Her rage boiled in her as Colin held her back, and she hissed at him when he tried to speak to her calmly.

"Ye cannae attack him, lass," he whispered.

"You know what he did! I don't have to say it, you know!" she gritted out through clenched teeth.

Colin looked in her eyes filled with rage and then embraced her in front of the whole clan. "Aye, I ken wha' he did, but now is no' the time or place fer wha' ye seek."

CHAPTER 25

"Why has he been allowed to continue living!" Audrina demanded.

Once the great hall doors were shut behind the soldiers, most of the people cleared out and went about their business. Word spread like wild fire of Cotswold's unexpected appearance, and they were sure to be spreading rumors about his reaction to Audrina.

The few remaining people in the hall looked between Colin and Audrina, before Colin turned and commanded, "Out w'it ye! Go aboot yer business!"

They hastened to leave with the exception of Mary, Donal and Alisdair.

"Alisdair, take Donal on a horse ride w'it Fergus, will ye?" Colin asked Alisdair.

"I doonae want tae go! I want tae stay here!" Donal protested.

"Nay lad, tis no' a conversation yer privy tae hear jest now," Colin commanded.

"But…" Donal protested.

"Out w'it ye, lad, and tha's an order or t'will be a lashing fer yer wayward tongue!" Colin roared.

Colin's anger seemed to break through some of Audrina's. She knew she was in another time, but she had never abided by the idea if beatings administered to a child.

"Colin…" she chastised.

"Och, I'm verra sorry, lad. Ye ken I'd ne'er lay a hand on ye, but I need tae speak w'it Maeve on this. Alone, aye?" His voice softened.

Donal looked between them, then nodded. He gave Colin a quick hug around the middle, and Colin in turn patted him on the head. What surprised Audrina was when Donal then squeezed her waist briefly. He usually ducked out of embraces.

"You'll no' let Cotswold take her again, will ye, Colin?" His innocent face was upturned to Colin as he asked the question that had been really burning in his heart.

"Nay, o'course I willnae. He cannae ha' her again. She belongs tae me," he told him firmly.

Donal finally seemed satisfied with this answer, because he got up and dutifully left the hall with Alisdair walking behind him.

Audrina began to walk the length of the main table with her hands behind her back. Her emotions were so intense, she didn't know how to begin. Colin and Mary watched her apprehensively before she paused in front of them and said,

"I've told you both my story. You know both sides of it, and I can't change what you may or may not believe. But what I don't understand is why that man has been allowed to continue murdering people. You saw the way he looked at Aine. If she has a prospective in her future, she is just as doomed as I, as Maeve was. You know, deep down he never just, 'let me go.' I didn't just wander off into that field. Yet why was Maeve's death not avenged? I know I'm asking you to stand on faith here, but I need an answer to this, please," she asked, looking between Mary and Colin.

"Because, tis no' tha' simple, lass. I lay broken and bleedin' aft Cotswold's men beat me down. It took me three days tae rise from me bed and when ye didnae return…we had little tae go on aboot where ye were. Certain, formalities are exchanged betwixt the Lords in the Highlands. As Laird o' the Claran clan, I had tae first formally make an inquiry tae Lord Cotswold's close friend and neighbor, Lord Weatherby. The courier was ri' quick w'it his messages, but there's a discretion amongst the English Lords. Although Cotswold isnae like outside his circle o'friends, the ones he is close tae will dismiss racism tae a certain level. The English look at us Scots as lesser beins.' E'en the Lairds among us. Aft Lord Weatherby informed us he didnae ken anything aboot murdered brides, he was fair certain tae believe his friend's word that they went missin' I set off for the ride tae Cotswold Castle. Aft that, it had been near a fortnight that ha' passed. When I arrived, Cotswold told me he had set ye loose, and ye had wandered off. T'was his word against mine and if I acted against him, he had and still has the right tae claim me lands and people tae do w'it as he sees fit."

Colin fell silent as Audrina digested the words. It seemed no matter what Colin did, he was never going to win against Cotswold. He could raise the highlands in search of her, but if Cotswold deemed it so, he could take everything from Colin that he had ever loved, including her.

"Colin was ready tae avenge ye, lass," Mary said quietly. "'Tis no' that I doonae love ye as me own, tis me tha' was the one tae convince him tae bring tae light all the evil that Cotswold has done, and no' at the price of his kin and home."

Audrina understood what Mary was saying. Colin would have given it all up had she not intervened. She couldn't bring herself to be mad at Mary for it. Were she in her shoes, she might have done the same thing.

She walked over to Mary and gave the woman's hand a squeeze. "There must be some way to bring Cotswold down," she mused out loud.

"We've thought of e'rything we can think of, lass, without the aid o'Weatherby…" he trailed off.

Audrina asked them, "What would happen if the murders were discovered? If Lord Weatherby learned of it and it was proven? Would he be tried and hanged?"

"Nay, the English favor their own. Most like, they would send him back tae London in exchange fer a less deranged relative. But e'en then, he's got powerful connections in London."

"But, so does Lord Weatherby right?"

"Aye, he does."

"So, it's worth a try then? It could be done?"

Audrina asked them. A small glimmer of hope began to shimmer in her chest. Justice in medieval times might not be fair, but if it were at all possible, she would seek it out, even if it was given in minute increments.

Colin began stroking his beard and Mary's eyes became unfocused as they both became lost in thought. They, if anyone, would know how to catch Cotswold in his treachery.

After a long moment, Colin said, "Aye, tis possible. But I doonae ken how we might go aboot doing it yet, lass, so doonae think on it anymore this day."

Audrina nodded, recognizing the topic was being dismissed.

Colin strode to a door on the side of the hall and called a command. Maids rushed in and began clearing the tables, as he had just given them leave to enter the hall again.

Audrina walked to the window and looked out. The day had formed into a beautiful day with a cool breeze to keep the hot rays of the sun at bay, and she didn't fancy spending the rest of it locked away in her chamber or cooped up in the tower.

"Colin," she called.

He had been standing with one of his men and issuing instructions. He looked up and held up a finger to indicate he would be with her in a moment. Mary had wandered off in search of her embroidery and Audrina waited near the window. After a few moments, Colin returned to her side with a puzzled look on his face.

"Aye, Maeve?" he asked.

"I was just wondering, if you have a lot to do today?" She bit her lip. She was sure he had a ton of responsibilities, and she didn't want him to shirk his duties, but after coming face to face with Cotswold, she needed the reassuring feel of his presence.

"I always have things tae do, lass, but what do ye need?" he asked.

"Oh, I don't want to bother you. It's alright," she tried to reassure him, but he didn't take the bait.

"Lass, I'd move mountains fer ye if it meant makin' ye happy. Movin' a wee bit o'me tasks isnae goin' tae cease the operations of runnin' the keep. What do ye need?" There was a twinkle in his eye as he told her this. His words caused a small blush to color her cheeks, and the quirk of his lips widened when he saw it.

"I was just wondering, if you have a horse, if you could teach me to ride, and maybe we could ride out and meet Donal?" she asked tentatively.

Her request seemed like a lot to her and she wouldn't mind if he couldn't. Her next request if he was too busy was to ask if she could tag along with him as he carried out his duties.

He looked surprised for a moment, but then amicable as he said, "Aye lass, I've a horse we can ride. T'will take too long tae teach ye tae ride. Donal and Alisdair will be back long afore yer seat holds enough tae ride on yer own, but ye can ride astride w'it me and me stallion."

Audrina nodded and secretly reveled in the opportunity to be so close to Colin. Luckily, she had on some trousers under her dress.

He led the way back out to the stable and introduced her to a great brown stallion named, Ewan. Audrina had doubts about her request when she saw the size of Ewan, but Colin stepped up to the horse and calmed him. He grabbed her hand and held it up, so the horse could catch her scent, and her fingers twitched when Ewan nuzzled her, and the softness of his muzzle, tickled her palm.

Colin led Ewan into the corridor and then grabbed Audrina around the waist. He lifted her with ease onto the back of the horse, and then used a block of wood to step up on and swing his own leg over the horse's back. Ewan seemed undeterred at the weight upon his back and set off at a brisk trot out into the courtyard. The gate keeper waved them on as they rode out, and multiple people waved at them as they passed through the streets of the town. Once they were clear, Colin allowed Ewan to open up into a long canter, which made the passing fields and forests blur by.

Audrina laughed as she became caught up in the adrenaline of the ride, and it wasn't long before she and Colin caught up to Donal and Alisdair. The pair of them looked at the two of them, but said nothing as they slowed to a walk alongside them, and Audrina realized, she didn't mind the warm feeling of Colin's palm pressed against her belly.

CHAPTER 26

T hat night, Audrina returned to her
chamber feeling refreshed but tired from
her bout of fresh air. It didn't take her
long to sink into a stupor in her aromatic bath
water. Audrina's thoughts were a jumble of how to
approach Lord Weatherby and convince him to
listen to her without accusing her of witchcraft and
recounting the fond memory of an afternoon spent
with Colin and his brothers. They had teased her
mercilessly and she had laughed alongside them.

They had ridden to a clearing in the woods and
Audrina recognized it as the area just before the cover
of the rowan trees where the pool formed in the
creek. They had paused and let the horses rest on the
banks of the creek and have a drink. They had wiled
away the afternoon hours, mostly in entertainment

watching Colin teach Audrina how to duel. She hadn't really dueled. Even young Donal had been able to best her because it took years of practice with a claymore or broadsword for someone to become skilled at sword fighting. They did teach her the grip that was necessary to hold a sword and Audrina found them to be quite heavy and difficult to pick up. Once her muscles determined she was not quitting, and quivered with exertion, they taught her a few thrusts with the sword, so that if she were ever attacked by the English, she would know where to strike.

"Does this mean I get my own sword?" she asked Colin hopefully.

He laughed and told her, "Nay, lass. I cannae risk ye cuttin' someone's head off w'it yer temper should they e'er displease ye. Mostly, mine tha' is."

"Well how am I supposed to thrust a sword into an Englishman, if he attacks me, if I don't have one?" she demanded with her hands on her hips.

"Because you willnae be havin' tae defend yerself. If ye meet a Sassenach, ye run like hell, while I protect ye." He laughed.

Audrina was unaccustomed to medieval chivalry or effeminizing ways. She had grown up learning to fend for herself. And although she had never been attacked with a sword, his words stung her pride a bit.

"I don't need a protector!" she declared, and he raised his eyebrows at her.

"Nay?" he asked.

"No. Besides, you weren't there to protect me when Cotswold…" she trailed off at the hurt look on his face. She'd wounded his pride and she hadn't meant to. "Colin, I'm sorry, that's not what I meant," she said quickly.

"I ken wha' ye were tryin' tae say, lass. And ye must believe me, I would ha'e raised Cotswold Castle tae get tae ye afore he harmed ye if I had been able."

"I know, Colin. I know." She walked up to him and out her hands on either side of his face. He had been sitting on a rock, close to where he and Maeve had been kissing the night she had the dream about him. His whole body bunched as his muscles tightened in anticipation. She bent low and kissed his forehead, offering a truce, but still remaining guarded. "Now, attack me," she commanded stepping back.

Donal and Alisdair snickered, but she raised an eyebrow at them.

"Are ye daft, lass?" Colin asked her. He didn't bother to move from his seat.

"Oh no. I'm very serious. I want to show you how I will defend myself sans a sword if I should be attacked by an Englishman again," she told him.

Colin and the others looked at her skeptically, but she shrugged off her tartan, in favor of the less cumbersome simple dress. She could still perform the moves she needed to in the dress to prove her point.

Colin got up and danced around a bit, clearly showing off, as he had no inkling of what she was about to do, and she suspected he thought he would easily better her in an instant. Up against brute strength, he was clearly the favored. That and with a sword, but she had a few moves that would at least bring him to his knees, so she could prove she had the opportune moment to scamper away if necessary. Sometimes all she needed was but a moment.

Colin clearly had no idea what was coming, nor did his brothers because they stared at her open-mouthed and wide-eyed when she used one of Colin's pressure points that she had learned about, courtesy of Mr. Tanaka's teachings. He began laughing when she demonstrated the move for him so that he might learn it, and they all rode back to the castle together, talking about battle techniques and strategies. The day had been a refreshing distraction from the more pressing matters that weighed heavily on her mind when she finally laid down to sleep.

After Audrina got out of the bath, she put on a slip of a nightgown and crawled into bed, letting her eyes flutter closed.

ತ⁊ಾ

SHE WAS LYING ON HER BACK WITH HER EYES closed, talking to the cows. She was in the stable, the rain had been lashing against the roof all afternoon and the cows were lying down in their stalls. She had wrapped herself in Colin's plaid for warmth and was singing and talking cheerfully when her eyes popped open, but only for the briefest moment as she felt the familiar kiss of Colin's mouth upon hers. Maeve smiled into his mouth as she deepened the kiss, and she felt his warm palm caress her stomach as it trailed along her thighs. It dipped under her skirt and slowly slid up her inner thighs as she moaned into his mouth. His fingers found her thatch of curls between her legs, she hated the restrictive pantaloons. He smiled in turn to discover her wicked indecency. Her legs parted as his fingers probed her wet folds. He stoked her in time with his tongue and she clung to his neck as he covered her body with his. He shielded her from discovery and she rode him like she fantasized about doing every night in the loneliness of her bed. She wasn't sure she could deny him any longer. He had been asking for her hand for months now and she had been denying him, but her resolve was waning the more he explored her body with his hands. The maddening thing was, he wouldn't let her touch him, apart from the contact through his trews, and he knew it drove her to the brink of madness. She desperately wanted to please him as he was her, and he denied her, claiming she could have all of him when she agreed to marry him. His fingers found the rhythm that drove her to the edge, and just as she was about to plummet over, he stayed his hand, causing her to whimper into his mouth.

"Colin, doonae stop, please!" she cried.

"Say it, lass, say ye'll have me. Tomorrow night. We'll wed in secret, so no one can ken o'our elopement," he persuaded her. "Say it and I'll give ye the touch ye need, lass."

He kissed her forehead and she nodded.

"Nay, say it. Say ye'll ha' me. Tell me ye love me," he urged.

"Och, Colin. Aye, I'll ha' ye. I'll wed ye because I love ye. Please!" she gasped.

His mouth closed over hers.

She screamed his name, "Colin!" as his fingers plummeted into her depths, shattering her soul into pieces as she gave herself up to him and in turn, he gave her the orgasm she desperately needed.

❦

AUDRINA AWOKE AND FOUND HERSELF CRYING Colin's name. "Colin! Colin, I need you!" she called.

He was there in an instant. Through the door and at her side.

"Lass, what is it? Wha's the matter?" he asked.

He checked her all over to see if she had been

harmed in some way, but she wrapped her arms around his neck, pulling him down to her. She initiated the kiss, delving her tongue into his surprised, open mouth.

He responded instantly, taking back control as he wrapped his hands around her waist and lifted her to him. Her fingers raked into his hair and he dragged his tongue down the column of her neck, tickling her with his beard.

Audrina gasped as his teeth found her collar bone, and he nipped his mark into her flesh. His hands roamed her back and bottom, and he dragged her shift up and over her head.

She clawed at his tartan, nearly strangling him in it in her haste to get it off, and he chuckled as he grabbed her wrists and held them wide, so he could stare down at her naked form. He stood her up and in front of him, so he could get a full look at her, never having seen his wife completely nude before. She shivered in anticipation to the hungry look her wore on his face as he stood and circled her.

He stood behind her and nuzzled her neck as his hands went from her shoulders down her arms and back up to cup her breasts. He lifted and squeezed them, playing with the mounds of flesh before letting his palms slide down her flat tummy and explore her curls between her legs. He found the same maddening rhythm as in her dream, and before too long she whirled in his arms, trying to claw off his kilt in an attempt to get to him.

He tugged at the knot near his shoulder and the whole ensemble fell to the floor in a piling heap of material, and when they stepped together, they shivered upon the contact of their skin on skin. Audrina's hand drifted southward and she wrapped her palm around his swollen erection. It pulsed in her hand as she stroked up and down, and he groaned, dropping his head into her shoulder.

"I cannae wait any longer, lass," he pleaded. "I have tae ha' ye now!" he demanded.

She nodded her head and he lifted her onto the bed and laid her down. His body followed hers, big, strong and powerful as he held himself above her, and his palm found her thighs, gently spreading them as he then pushed first with one knee, then both. She was so ready for him, but as she glanced between them, she was worried because he was so big.

He smiled, reassuringly when he guessed at her apprehension, and his fingers found her center again, stroking her to readiness. When he felt that she was, he slowly pushed forward, and her tightness engulfed him. He kissed away her moans and soft whimpers as she worked to relax around him. He was ever patient as he had always been with her, and when he breeched her maidenhood, he was careful not to cause unnecessary pain.

"How" he whispered.

"Magic," she said with a smile.

Audrina breathed rapidly as her body clenched around him. He was filling her up in a way she had never thought possible. He stilled when he made the final thrust into her and allowed her to grow accustomed to him. But all too soon, the neediness erupted in her again, and she needed him to move.

He started slow, with long, easy strokes as he worked himself in and out of her. She could feel the exertion it took him to retain so much control, by the way his muscles quivered under her touch. She wondered at how it must have felt for him to be denied what he wanted for so long, content to tease Maeve until she gave in to him, only to have her snatched away the night he thought he would be rewarded for his patience with this very act. She urged him to take what he needed, faster and faster with her hips.

His resolved cracked at the same time the pressure of her need met his. He lost himself in her as she spiraled out of control around him. He plunged into her for the last time as she quaked around him in an earth shattering orgasm. She felt himself spill over into her and then collapse on top of her. He was careful not to crush her, but pulled her to his chest when he turned on his side. They laid there breathing together until the draw of sleep pulled them both under.

When Audrina woke the next morning, she discovered she was shocked that she held no reservations about calling to Colin the night before. She was content as she laid in his arms and watched him sleep.

CHAPTER 27

Colin woke a few moments after Audrina did, to the touch of her fingers on his face.

"Good morrow." He smiled down at her warmly.

"Good morning," she murmured. She stretched, unsure of how she would feel after her first time, and found she was only slightly sore, less than she had expected to be.

"Are ye alright, lass?" he asked as he stretched out onto his back and tucked an arm under his head.

"Yes, I'm fine thank you." She stared down at him awkwardly. She felt the color in her cheeks begin to rise, and she looked away from him as she contemplated what she should say next.

"No' havin' second thoughts are ye, lass? I can prove tae ye tha' ye need no' be distressed."

"How are you going to do that?" she wondered out loud before she shrieked when he tackled her.

He was just as gentle the second time as he was the first, accounting for the fact that she was sore. When she awoke the second time, he laughed at her when they both heard her stomach emit a great gurgling sound.

"Hungry, Maeve?" he asked.

She blinked a minute and then nodded her head. It was stills strange to her to be called Maeve, even though she knew she had been her in her previous life.

"I'll go and see if I can find somat tae eat fer ye." He rolled out of bed.

Audrina clung to the sheet and hugged it up around her chin as she watched him pad around the bed like a great predatory beast.

He made a show of bending down to pick up his kilt, which made her eyes widen as she got a view of him and his, 'goods' as he stood up and then folded the material, so he could begin wrapping it around his waist.

He needn't have bothered, because when he went to the door of the chamber and opened it, he discovered that a tray of food had been left for them of breads, cheeses, fruits and dried meats. Audrina continued to clutch the sheet around her as he unpinned his kilt and climbed back into bed. He settled her on his lap, as the bed was narrow, and she was painstakingly aware of him pressed between them. The rasp of him tickled her hip and she squirmed in his arms.

"If ye doonae hold still, lass, I'll no' be able tae concentrate on feedin' ye breakfast, and then yer stomach will be growlin' at me again," he teased her.

Audrina stilled in his arms and resolutely refused to look him in the face. She could feel him smiling down at the top of her head, and she wondered if she would ever overcome her shyness and embarrassment.

Audrina picked at the cheese and the fruit, and then she tore off a piece of bread, turning it over in her fingers.

"Where does the grain come from for the bread in the castle?" she asked.

The question surprised him, but he shrugged his curiosity at the sudden question off and answered, "Tis from a field out past the farmer's. A man named Raibert farms the fields and o'ersees the farm."

"Does he also sell the grain in the market-place?" she wondered.

"Aye, he does. Why, lass?" he asked as he bit into his own bread.

"I think I saw him. The day I first came here. He was selling to another man and the man accused him of overcharging for it. I noticed the grain was mixed with the previous year's stock."

Colin stilled as he listened to her words. "Are ye sure, lass, tis an offense tae cheat me people. Raibert can be fined a sum for his dishonesty."

"Well, I don't want to get anyone in trouble, Colin. But I did see two men and they did talk about that. I would have to see him to know if it were him or not," she replied. She suddenly felt very uncomfortable, but Colin kissed her nose.

"Doonae be upset for tellin'. Tis the mark o'a good Lady to her Laird. She's supposed tae be quiet and observant, all traits ye possess. T'will be yer duty tae see things I doonae, or notice slights o'hand if I am tae busy w'it other aspects o'the keep. Doonae worry yerself o'er the man. He'll be fined, but no' punished harshly. I'm no' barbaric like the English."

Audrina felt better at these words. She had never meant to tell on purpose, it was just one of those things that didn't sit well with her, and she had been trying to rid her mind of any trivial anxieties, so that she could cope with the bigger issues. She wanted a clear mind when she formulated a plan to convince Lord Weatherby that Lord Cotswold was a treacherous murderer.

"Mayhap I should go and speak w'it them now," Colin pondered.

"No, please stay." Audrina was drawn from her own thoughts.

"Aye?" he asked.

"Umm, yes. This is, well this is nice. It's like the honeymoon that we never got. You and Maeve that is," she stammered. She tried not to look away when her cheeks flamed, but under the intensity of his gaze, she looked at the window.

Colin cupped her chin and tilted her head up. "You'll ne'er be judged by me fer the things ye ask fer or need, lass," he said softly. "That includes anything ye might be feelin' here in our marriage bed."

He brought his lips to hers and she sighed as she felt part of her hesitancy leave her body. She could grow accustomed to this, mornings spent waking up in Colin's arms.

Part of her wanted to pinch herself just to make sure it wasn't all just a really good dream. But deep down in her soul she knew without a shadow of a doubt, it wasn't a dream, and this was somehow the place she was supposed to be. Right here, right now.

"Well, at the risk of ruining that sentiment," she murmured into his lips, "we need to talk about the chapel." She felt Colin stiffen and she knew she had touched on a nerve. He sat back and looked at her warily.

"Aye?" he asked.

"Yes," she responded. "I know it's where it all happened. Where Cotswold beat you. I know it's where you were betrayed, but Colin, the chapel is important. One priest who betrayed you shouldn't make you shut out the place forever. You have a priest here, I've seen him around the keep. Why not let him use the chapel?" she pressed.

"Because, it's no' aboot the priest betrayin' me. Tis aboot being the place tha' I lost ye, and some-times' I thought I'd lost ye forever," he admitted.

Audrina sat back and looked at him. He was so sincere, and he truly believed it was somehow cursed or something. Like the fairy rings scattered around Scotland, Colin had the adamant belief that the chapel, was somehow the grounding force that was responsible for the disappearance of his Maeve. She could understand that. But she also knew that his fear stemmed from the knowledge that he had pushed Maeve to get married. He had been the one to urge her to go on with the ceremony, when she had reservations not about him, but about the marriage rights that came after. Cotswold had weaponized those rights and in doing so, he had driven a wedge in between Colin's faith and faith in the sanctimony of marriage.

Audrina closed her fingers in Colin's and brought his hand to her lips. She was holding his left hand and she bent down and placed a kiss on his ring finger where a wedding band should be resting. "He doesn't have me now, Colin. I'm right here and I'm not going anywhere," she promised.

Colin sucked in a harsh breath and for the first time, she noticed the struggle in his eyes as he held back unshed tears over the loss of his wife. She smoothed her palm over his cheek and he bent his head to kiss it as she crooned to him. She wasn't aware, but she began singing to him, the old Scottish folk song that her grandfather used to sing.

He swayed slightly at her words and she finished the song.

"Ye've always had a beautiful voice, lass," he murmured into her palm. He blinked his eyes open and she found them clear again. "E'en when ye were singing to the coos."

She chuckled at this and realized it would be just like her to do such a thing. She'd never heard of the phrase, cow whisperer, but she'd always been a fan of the novel "The Horse Whisperer" by Nicholas Evans. The book had been dear to her, one that she had been a fan of for its simple romance story. That made her wonder, "Colin, is there a library here?"

His brow furrowed, and she rephrased her question.

"Are there books here?" she asked.

A dawning look came across his face and he smiled. "Aye, books are scarce as many cannae read, but there are a few aboot the keep. I'll ha'e some rounded up fer ye."

"Oh, thank you!" she proclaimed and leaned up to kiss him.

He pulled back and had a puzzled look on his face.

"What?" she asked.

"I didnae ken ye could read is all," he said.

She laughed and replied, "One of the many mysteries Colin MacClaran will have to discover of his strange wife, Audrina and Maeve MacClaran."

He thought about this a moment and then shrugged, obviously not caring anymore if she still believed she was from the future.

"Aye, and the first thing I learned from ye, lass, is tha' if I apply a wee bit o'pressure just here," he grasped her wrists and pushed her gently toward the mattress so she was on her stomach. Without hurting her, he pinned her arms behind her back, and climbed on top of her and leaned down to whisper in her ear, "then I can ha'e ye in a most accommodating position of me liking."

He thrust up into her, causing her to gasp in pleasure at the new sensation. The afternoon was spent in similar compromising positions as they explored one another, until a shout rang through the courtyard.

"Lord Cotswold and Lord Weatherby, hereby proclaim that the witch known as Maeve MacClaran, be brought before them to be tried and judged per their discretion!"

CHAPTER 28

Colin rose from bed so rapidly that Audrina stumbled as she numbly got out of bed herself. He hastened to wrap his plaid around him and she pulled her dress on. Audrina heard footsteps in the corridors, running toward the sounds of the shouts. She glanced out the window and gasped when she saw the courtyard full of English soldiers.

"T'will be alright, lass," Colin said hastily, but even she knew how dire the situation was. He rushed to her, glancing out at the courtyard at the two riders who were surrounded by guards and sitting astride the finest steeds.

Colin turned Audrina away from the window. "I willnae let tha' man ha' ye again. I made a promise tae ye and I will keep it."

Audrina nodded as he kissed her, and then they walked to the door.

Mary ran up to them with Donal and Alisdair. "Och, Colin, wha' will ye do?" she cried.

"I'll go down and meet them," he replied.

"I'm ready tae fight w'it ye!" Donal cried brandishing his small dirk.

"Aye, I ken ye are. But I need ye tae stay and protect our mam."

Donal looked as if he was going to protest, and then he looked at his mother who clutched him to her.

"Aye, I will. Upon me honor!" He thumped his skinny chest and Audrina felt her lips twitch despite the direness of the situation.

Colin looked at his mother. "Lock yerselves below until we come tae get ye. If we've no' come by dawn tomorrow, use the tunnels tae run and make yer escape. Go tae Skye, we've allies there who will take ye in."

Mary looked as if she was going to protest, but Colin stepped in, kissing her cheek. Alisdair, did the same and then Colin turned to him.

"See that there's a group o'men on the tower, ready w'it arrows and a group along the walls. Ha'e a group waiting here to come in upon me signal, should the meeting turn fer the worst. Make sure the townsfolk are secured, send a few men out tae show them the escape through the mountains and the caves should the English o'er run the castle."

Alisdair embraced Colin in a hug and then bowed to Audrina as he ran off with his sword drawn. He bellowed commands in Gaelic to the Scottish men who roused to their stations in anticipation of taking on the English troops.

Colin took Audrina by the elbow. "Ye ready, lass?"

"As ready as I'll ever be," she told him wringing her hands.

She was anxious, as she hadn't had time to properly formulate a plan to convince Lord Weatherby of her innocence and convict Lord Cotswold of murder. It would be Lord Cotswold's word against hers, and from what she knew of witch trials, the accused was rarely given a fair trial. And what constituted as fair was often done at the pain and torture of the witch who was out through various tests to determine if she was a witch or not. In the unlikely event she did survive the trails and tests and came out of them unharmed and unscathed, her own people often turned on her for having the fortitude to survive and killed her or banished her anyway. Audrina felt a wave of nausea wash over her.

Colin cupped her face. "Breathe, lass, breathe," he coaxed her.

Audrina couldn't help but wonder what horrible torture they had in store for her. She wondered if she could somehow call the magic that Maeve had, but realized she had no idea how to.

"I'm alright," she told him. "Really, you're here. It will all be alright somehow."

Colin nodded as he steered her to the front doors of the great hall. There was no telling what would happen once they confronted the English Lords, but Audrina was grateful she had been graced the one night with Colin if this was to be the end. She recalled the memory and feel of him on top of her and in her. She took solace in the strength that emitted from his powerful body, because he had shown her that strength himself. Audrina placed in the forefront of her mind, the pictures he had sketched for her. The things she loved and she held important were her strength, as was Colin.

Colin's men flanked him, and they proceeded to march out the front door and confront her accusers. Audrina was relieved slightly that she had Colin by her side. She had no doubt he would lay down his life to protect her, and that he would never let Cotswold harm her again. Audrina palmed the pin of her kilt, wondering if the spell would work a second time through the ages or if it had been a one-time deal if she was torn from him in this life again.

Colin laced his fingers with hers as he kept his hand on his sword. As they descended the steps, she was glad to see he held his head high, not being cowed by Lord Weatherby and Lord Cotswold sitting astride their horses.

When they came to about fifteen paces between them and the Lords, Colin called out, "Why have ye come tae accuse me wife o'witchcraft? What evidence d'ye ha'e o'the allegation?"

Lord Cotswold urged his horse a few paces forward, but it was Lord Weatherby that Audrina's attention was fixated on. He was tall and fit with carrot blond hair and dressed conservatively which was in stark contrast to Lord Cotswold. His intense gray eyes were fixed on her and she would first describe him as looking down on everyone he came across, accept the appearance was precipitated by his overly large nose. He turned his attention from her to Colin as Colin asked his question.

Lord Cotswold drew her attention when he pointed a finger at her and shouted, "She's an imposter, a monster, a witch! Maeve MacClaran is dead!"

Audrina didn't know what to say to these accusations, but Colin was quick to think.

He began laughing, openly at Lord Cotswold. She was worried at first that his mockery of Lord Cotswold would be met with a swift death, but apparently being a Laird, even a Scottish one held some merit as it stayed the swords of the soldiers and he men. She was still unsure of what his motivations were to make a mockery of Lord Cotswold and she looked up at him, in hopes of some sign of his plan. She was confused at first until the nervous twitterings began to emit from the men around her. He grasped her under the elbow and took a few paces toward Lord Cotswold. At first, she resisted, not wanting to be anywhere nearer to her murderer than she had to be, but then he turned them in a circle so that all the Scotsmen and Englishmen could see her.

"Aye? Maeve MacClaran is dead, ye say? This woman here?" he called loudly so everyone could hear him.

A low rumbling of comments and whispers

passed through the watching crowd. Audrina noticed the few townspeople who had been in the courtyard, slowly make their way to the great hall to barricade themselves in. She hoped they had the forethought to run and hide if they had the chance, and that they knew of the secret passages that Colin had told his mother about. She hated to think that any of them would be trapped in the keep with no escape, and all because of her.

Lord Cotswold turned to his men and they fell silent under his withering stare. "She's an imposter then. A witch!" he roared.

Some of the men looked nervously at her, but she held her chin high as Colin once again called out Lord Cotswold on his claims.

"What evidence d'ye ha'e?"

Lord Cotswold opened his mouth and shut it, looking at Lord Weatherby.

Lord Weatherby raised his eyebrows, but continued to say nothing. He was clearly waiting for Lord Cotswold's proof himself or give an indication that Lord Cotswold was calling his men to arms on behalf of England if the Scots attacked first. Lord Weatherby looked bored at best, despite his calculating eyes giving away that he was paying attention to every detail.

Audrina was beginning to feel a spark of hope, that maybe Lord Weatherby could be reasoned with, when the sound of marching and wagon wheels approaching captured her attention. She, along with the rest of the men in the courtyard, turned to the open gate, to watch a procession of soldiers filter in through the gate.

Audrina turned back to Lord Cotswold who had a nasty smile on his face when he watched her as the soldiers moved in. Audrina's heart began to thump loudly as she realized, the procession was the accumulation of more English soldiers, outnumbering the Scottish men at least three to one.

Audrina watched as the soldiers wheeled the horse drawn cart into the center of the courtyard and brought it to a halt. The soldiers jumped down from the wagon and marched around the back, drawing back a cover and revealing the contents that lay inside.

Audrina was confused for a moment as she tried to discern what she was looking at. At first, they unloaded two long wooden planks that two soldiers began to secure together. Next, they unloaded the cartons full of wood and dried heather, and Audrina gasped in horror as she realized what it was they were doing.

Colin tensed next to her and squeezed her hand in reassurance as the English soldiers continued to set up the pyre that would be used to burn her at the stake as a witch. Of all the ways Audrina had imagined she might be tried and executed as a witch, this was the worst in her opinion. From what she had read of the executions, the accused suffered unmeasurable pain and screamed until the heat left their voices too raw and they passed out from the pain. The heat was what reached the victims first, not the flames. And it was an agonizing process for the victims as it boiled them in their own skins. Audrina tried to breathe as she felt the panic attack begin.

"Again, I ask wha' yer proof is that me wife is a witch," Colin demanded in a cold hard voice.

Audrina felt the heat from the sun beating down on her, and she thought she was going to pass out. Only the pressure of Colin's hand on hers was enough to keep her from fainting.

CHAPTER 29

"I demand ye cease this at once!" Colin shouted at the English soldiers. His voice was terrifying, and Audrina flinched under the enormity of the rage of it. The English soldiers pause in securing the two pieces of wood into the cross and look between Lord Cotswold and Lord Weatherby. The men who were stacking the wood and scattering it with the dried Heather, also pause as the other soldiers who are lined up in formation look around nervously.

"You will do as you were ordered!" Lord Cotswold hollered at them.

The men pause, but only for a moment as they looked at Lord Weatherby. He made no indication one way or another, so they slowly began to continue the setup of the pyre.

Audrina concentrated on not fainting, and she looked around desperately. The men on the walls were tense and ready, waiting for Colin's command. She felt the presence behind her of the personal guard that Colin had brought with them, but what really surprised her was when she glanced toward the chapel, and saw a flicker of movement in the small, plain windows. It appeared as if Alisdair had the forethought to position some men hidden away so that if necessary, they could ambush the unsuspecting Lord Cotswold by rushing his horse. With any luck, there unknown presence would spook the Lord's horse and cause it to throw him, and they could capture him in exchange for Lord Weatherby to call off his men.

Audrina shook her head, not wanting to give their position away and she turned her attention back to Lord Cotswold and Colin.

"Where is your priest to test her?" Colin sneered. "I figured it would be Father Graham, the man you paid to betray me a year ago when you took her."

"I was acting under the rights of Prima Noctem, as you well know when I informed you a year ago. It was my right to take her. As for Father Graham, I told you when I occupied Cotswold

Castle that I have emissaries everywhere to keep me apprised of the happenings between my charges and duties."

Colin seemed to mull this over, carefully considering who he was to be able to trust now. He had made it a priority to befriend as many people as he could throughout the region in order to be apprised himself of the English occupancy, and his secret plot to eventually overthrow Lord Cotswold could be the very reason the Lord singled him out and taunted him so much. Ever since Lord Cotswold had come to Scotland, he and Colin had barely maintained civility. Cotswold made it a point to taunt Colin as much as he could, showing up at Claran Castle whenever he felt. He would often impose unfair taxes that left the Claran estate in dire jeopardy of not being able to maintain itself. But Colin had grown wise to his scheming ways, and secreted away monies and food stores to see his people through the hard winters. Cotswold had long suspected Colin of doing as such, and had been harassing him ever since.

"Whose authority are ye acting on now?" Colin demanded.

"I am acting upon the authority of the English crown!" Lord Cotswold cut him off. "Anyway, I have no need, I am permitted to act of my own discretion and authority and I have first-hand knowledge that Maeve MacClaran is dead. This woman is a witch and by the teachings of the scripture, thou shalt not suffer a witch to live! She's cast you under her spell Colin MacClaran, it may be too late for you as well." He sneered down at him.

According to Lord Cotswold, the only good Scotsmen was a dead one of what Audrina had gathered from reading the brochure at the museum. That is to say, between the lines. He took pleasure in torturing Scotsmen and murdering them. He got away with it more with men because they were more likely to fight back, giving him the perfect excuse to say that they had attacked a Lord of England who was protected under the law of the crown. The brides he murdered were a trickier thing to deal with, as he had less excuses to cover for the atrocities he performed on them.

"I'm under no spell, Cotswold, an' tha's the truth o'it!" Colin barked.

"Careful, Claran, I think your impudence could do with a reminder that you serve the English crown. Perhaps a whipping from the Lord, that is to you, that you have affronted is just what you need to remember your place!" Cotswold's face was purple with rage.

Colin seemed to know how to get to him and enrage and goad him.

Cotswold turned his horse in a circle, away from Colin, giving Colin the opportunity to move back with Audrina a few paces. If things turned for the worst, he needed to be as close to the keep so he could aid Audrina in a swift escape and then take his place to defend the innocent lives hiding within his keep. Cotswold didn't seem to notice as he turned back around, sneering at Colin and Audrina as she watched the progress of the pyre being built.

"Is the witch afraid?" Cotswold goaded her.

She recalls the memory of Maeve standing up to him and fighting him off on her own in the tower. She picked her head up and looked him dead in the eye. "If I am to die on that fire, just know, I will find a way back. I will haunt you to the end of your days and drive you to madness. I will chase you into the fires of hell where your soul will be tortured for eternity as it burns along with mine." Audrina took a step toward him, but Colin held her back with a hand on her arm. She had spoken low enough so that only Lord Cotswold could hear her, and she made sure Cotswold alone saw the smile of determination on her face as she courageously stood her ground against her murderer and rapist.

Lord Cotswold snarled, sending spittle running down his fat chin, as he leered down at her so only she could hear him.

"I will find ecstasy in hearing the screams of your pain, witch. Just as I did that night a year ago." He shivered as he closed his eyes in memory.

Audrina backed away in disgust as she realized he was remembering the night and getting sexual pleasure from it. Her revulsion for that man knew no depths. It was as bottomless as his depravity.

Audrina was pulled back by Colin and they backed away as Colin's men brandished their swords at the English soldiers. Audrina noticed the men along the walls of the keep, aim their arrows at them and they held their position until the order was given.

"You don't want to do this, Laird MacClaran," Lord Weatherby finally called.

All attention turned to him and Colin froze.

"Ye leave me no choice if ye willnae give me wife a fair trial, Lord Weatherby. I beseech ye tae see reason. He's provided no evidence tha' she's a witch, and I willnae stand by and watch her be taken from me again at his hands. I beg ye to see reason. Ye've been a fair Lord o'er yer subjects through Scotia, and many ha'e favored ye to Lord Cotswold's rule. Let me speak w'it ye in private o'er the matter," Colin begged him. He was clearly not so proud that he wouldn't beg on her behalf, and she knew what price it came with at the cost of his pride.

Lord Weatherby seemed to mull this over a bit, but Lord Cotswold turned to him in a purple rage.

"Would you take the word of a Scotsman over your own countryman? I've come to you with the evidence, will you not stand your ground, these Scotsmen threaten you!" He cast a beefy arm in the direction of Colin's men.

When next he spoke he spoke gravely, "Lord Colin, Lord Cotswold's words ring true enough. Your men are posed to attack and that can only be seen as hostility to the crown. Lord Cotswold has been a long-standing friend, as well as his family to mine in London. Although I may not always agree with his more ruthless methods, as I favor diplomacy, he acts in accordance to the actions taken against him. As I see before me an openly hostile band of Scotsmen, I find myself bound by honor to take his word on the matter."

Cotswold turned back to them with a cold smile

on his face that sent shivers throughout her body. Lord Weatherby turned his horse and slowly circled around behind the pyre, placing himself in a position of authority to command his troops from the rear.

Colin didn't say another word to Cotswold, there was no need to. He pushed Audrina toward the steps and unsheathed his sword from his waist.

"It begins then, Cotswold, if ye continue tae pursue yer actions of buildin' tha' pyre and takin' me wife!"

Cotswold laughed, and his men closed ranks around him, as the standoff began. Audrina didn't need to hear Colin issue the order, she turned on the steps and ran to the door, as Colin's men shot flaming arrows at the courtyard. When she turned back, she noticed the arrows weren't in fact targeted at the English soldiers but hit in arcs at a semicircle in front of Colin and his men, lighting an arc of flame that acted as a barrier between the two troops.

The English backed away from the flames as Cotswold's horse reared. Audrina had hoped the horse would throw him back into the fire, but she could see his face enraged in the hazy smoke on the other side of the flames. She hadn't anticipated, and neither had Cotswold, that Colin had the fore-thought and cleverness to soak the stones and ground at the base of the keeps doors to protect them from an attack such as this. She wondered what else her husband's clever mind had lent itself to in the way of battle tactics and fortifications. As she ran with him and locked herself in the keep, she was grateful that she had escaped murder at the hands of Lord Cotswold, a second time.

CHAPTER 30

Audrina watched as the men barricaded the door. Colin stepped down into the great hall and began issuing orders to fortify the castle against the impending attack. Audrina tried to stay out of his way, but the more she heard him command his men as if they were going to war, the more her panic increased. She felt the room begin to swirl around her and she sat down hard in one of the chairs. The men had worked on clearing most of the chairs and tables to the side of the room, so that they could take a defensive position with room to fight in the great hall if they needed too.

Audrina saw doors that had been previously locked and store rooms that she'd seen rarely delved into thrown open with gusto and the contents inside emptied out into the hall. She watched as four men lifted the main table out of the way, and the rug underneath kicked aside as a latch that had hidden a trap door underneath, was lifted. Swords and dirks where passed around. She saw claymores, broadswords and even imported steel from other countries that she knew wasn't native to Scotland. Colin had obviously prepared for a day such as this when the attack on the castle might happen. She watched as a particularly nasty and gleaming battle ax was handed off to Alisdair.

He happened to catch her eye and then tapped Colin's arm and pointed to her. She must have had a look on her face, because Colin issued a few more orders and then without a word, strode over to her, scooping her up in his arms and carried her upstairs. She only thought to protest him leaving his men to prepare when they were halfway up the stairs.

"Colin, you can't leave them. You have to lead your men!" she insisted.

"Haud yer wheest, woman!" He kissed her hard.

Audrina felt her panic increase to a dangerous level to the point that she was almost hyperventilating. Colin threw open the door to their chamber and carefully laid her on the bed. He strode over to the window and pulled the latch shut, effectively blocking any noise that would filter up through the open window.

"Colin…" she began to protest, but her panic had reached dangerous heights. He laid down on the bed beside her and pulled her to him. He crooned into her hair, and by the steady beat of his heart, guided her to find the calmness that he was emanating. He tilted her chin up and kissed her, making her forget about the men outside or the impending battle. He took her breath away on a level that exceeded the panic and she found it pleasant to become lost in him in a way that forced her mind to forget about becoming lost to her fear.

He didn't undress her this time, but Colin rose and tucked his own kilt up, baring himself to her. He raised her skirt and gently parted her, pushing into her in earnest. She was so ready for him. Wet with need and hungry for solace. Their lovemaking was fast and urgent, as was their call to arms in a few short hours. Audrina cried out in pleasure and pain at the onslaught of her fear. Colin knew he hadn't hurt her. He found his own release and subsequent fulfillment of her before he cradled her into his arms. Their lovemaking was a testament that, no matter what the circumstances were, even the pressure of war, their love would come first. She had needed him, and he filled her. He had needed her, and she accepted him into her, a receptacle for his love.

Audrina felt the tears cascade down her cheeks when it was over. It was enough and yet not enough. She could have stood to go another two rounds with him in his arms, but he had the responsibility now of protecting not only her, but his people as well. She knew this to be true, which is why it was heart-wrenching to force herself to tear away from his arms, so that he might not feel obligated to stay.

"Colin, I want you to know."

"Nay lass, tell me aft!" he pleaded.

The look on his face told her that wouldn't be able to bear her words of parting. She had not had the opportunity to say them the first time when Cotswold had stolen Maeve from him. And he had clearly tortured himself over thinking of all the things they might have said had they been given the opportunity.

"No, listen to me, Colin. I wanted to tell you that, no one has stood up for me in this way. Not since my grandfather was alive. I know there is question as to who he is to me and when he is, but the point is, before I came to you, came back to you, I had no one. These last couple of weeks have been a whirlwind, but there has been one certainty through it all, and that's you Colin. I love you, Colin MacClaran. I want you to take that with you when you go out there to face that monster," she finished. She'd never told him she loved him. She said it now with all the conviction within her soul and Maeve's. In doing so, it erased all lingering doubts she had in her mind. It washed away her fears and insecurities and the endless questions that seemed to barrage her mind and plague her thoughts. Whatever happened, if Cotswold won or they did, her love for Colin was certain and absolute.

Colin rose and went to her. "Aye, I love ye tae. I've always loved ye and I'll no' e'er stop lovin' ye, e'en if it means lovin' ye from heaven should me soul rest there fer eternity aft this night."

Audrina felt the tears slip down her cheeks and she leaned up on her toes and kissed him. She had precipitated so few of the kisses, and she made the third vow to herself. If God or whatever power deemed it necessary to return her Colin to her that night, she would be sure to kiss him every day until the end of their days in order to show him that love.

She leaned back and glanced out the window. She caught sight of Lord Weatherby and cursed. Colin raised his eyebrows, never having heard her curse before, and it caught him by surprise.

"What vexes ye, lass?" he asked.

"If only there was a way to make Lord Weatherby see." She chewed on her lip. "Cotswold is a slippery eel. If we could just show Weatherby what a lying, murdering…" she trailed off looking pensive.

"Lass, what is it. Out w'it it!" Colin gave her shoulders a little shake.

"That's it, Colin. He has lied!" she exclaimed excitedly.

"Aye, we ken it, but…" he trailed off, catching up with her train of thought.

"It would be the ultimate downfall of Cotswold, if we point out that he has always claimed the brides he has taken by rights of Prima Noctem got lost on the way home. He claimed he never knew what happened to me, but how would he have known I had died if he didn't know what happened to the brides?" Audrina's words came out in a rush.

Colin's brow lifted in concentration. "T'will be

tricky and risky tae call him out on it wit'out bein' shot at by arrows, lass," he commented.

"Tricky yes, but you're an expert at goading him. What if, you start by goading him? Burn the stake that he has set up. Make sure you have their undivided attention. Although I don't think that will be an issue, you need to make sure you capture the attention of Lord Weatherby as well. You need to get Cotswold good and enraged and then…"

"Then when he loses control o'er himself, he'll confess all in front o'Lord Weatherby, in an attempt tae save face!" Colin finished her sentence.

"Exactly!" she cried.

Colin dragged her to him and pulled her into another embrace and kiss. Together they had seen themselves through the denial of their love, a secret wedding, the agony of being wrenched apart and lost to one another, the torture of murder and despair and then the confusion and chaos of being thrust back together by a spell that neither could comprehend. They had endured the almost insur-mountable task of trusting one another again, and finally realizing and professing their love for one another all over again. With each other, they real-ized they could do anything.

When they broke free, she and Colin rushed to

the door. He paused a moment and turned, "Lass, I think ye should go to me mam and let me call Cotswold on…"

"Don't even think about excluding me from this, Colin MacClaran. I may be a woman, but I've faced the fires of hell at the hands of that man, I will not miss this opportunity to be avenged." She stamped her foot for emphasis, and he stepped back in surprise at the vehemence on her face.

"Alrigh', woman. Ye've made yer point. I'll no' deny ye." He snorted at the fiery flush in her cheeks and then opened the door. "But ye'll stay betwixt yer personal guard when we march out tae face him. Deal?" He held out his hand. It was her turn to snort in mirth as he bargained with her for the security and feeling of having the upper hand.

"Deal," she agreed, and she shook it.

Colin kissed the top of her hand, then he pulled a small dirk from the sheath on his belt and handed it to her. T'was yers when ye arrived from Skye. T'was yer sister, Catriona's. I kept it, but ye should ha' it if ye intend tae walk w'it me into battle. I suspect my men will see ye tae safety if our plan doosnae work, but tis a good weapon if ye use yer moves ye taught me yesterday on the ride out to Donal and Alisdair."

Audrina took the dirk and a flash of a face that resembled her own went through her mind. Catriona's. She was smiling at her, and for the briefest moment, the dirk warmed in her palm under her fingers. It felt right in her hand. It felt like it belonged.

CHAPTER 31

A lot of activity buzzed in the great hall when they came back downstairs. Colin began barking orders again, and Audrina was left standing to the side and waiting for the time when they would march out. She looked down at the dirk and discovered it to be gem encrusted with the same gems as on her kilt pin. She touches the pin, finding solace in the weight of it hanging near her shoulder. The dirk felt equally as comforting. Back in San Francisco, she had carried a can of pepper spray, and she always felt a mild sense of security when she had it, but nothing like the assurance of a weapon that could be lethal to the attacker who was trying to kill her. Pepper spray had been used to ward off an attack long enough to run away. It felt like to Audrina that she had been running away for a very long time. But this dirk meant that she didn't have to run anymore. She could stand up to what and who she feared and be brave in the face of adversity and staggering odds.

Audrina had never understood the pride that she had inherited from her Scottish ancestors. It was always joked about, her stubbornness and proud attitude. She understood it now. With only a few years before the Scots would as a whole, stake their claim against the English and proudly proclaim their independence as a free nation, she could see why that feeling inflated within her chest and made her feel like she was standing for something worth fighting for, something she believed in.

Audrina had the strangest feeling that, even though he wasn't born yet, or had been deceased for many years now, the soul of her grandfather was with her and basking in the pride she was emulating. He had understood it. He had known the people and the lands that were rich with history, culture, love and life was something unique to Scotland. Audrina hadn't fully understood this when they had poured over the many books. She had always known Grandfather missed the highlands. But with a young girl to take care of, and the responsibility to her and his own life, he had never returned to his homeland.

"Grandfather, if you can hear me, I promise you I will travel to Skye. I will see the land you came from, that I came from and I will bask in the beauty and magnitude of the magic that can be found there," she prayed to her grandfather.

A spark of hope lit her chest as he answered her in his own way. She knew without a shadow of doubt, she was home. Scotland was and always would be her home. She felt the fernweh and wanderlust settle and cease within her soul, as she realized she had found what she had been looking for. She looked at Colin who was going over the plan with his men.

"Are ye mad?" Alisdair asked him.

"Aye, mayhap a little, but it's our last chance," he told Alisdair.

Some of the men grumbled, but Colin silenced them with a wave.

"We've no' the resources or allies at our aid this eve tae take on all o'them," he reasoned.

One man called from the back, "Aye, but it could be the chance we have tae take down the murderous Sassenach!"

A chorus of cheers erupted, but Colin again

held his hand up. "Aye, we could. But we've learnt tha' attacking them only sees our men hanged by the noose. We could kill Cotswold tonight, or we could beat him at his own game. I'll no'deny my brothers, the day o'reckonin' is comin' fer the English, but it isnae tonight. Weatherby will be forced tae retaliate if we kill Cotswold outright. We cannae stand a chance against his armies alone. If we need tae, we'll gather the clans and make our stand. There's already talks of it ye ken tha' well enough. Tonight is aboot takin' back the MacClaran pride that he stole from us." Colin pointed to Audrina who gasped.

It had never occurred to her that the assault Cotswold had performed against her, was just as much an affront to the MacClaran people and men, as she was their Laird's wife. She stepped forward and held her head high as she addressed them.

"My fellow Claran's, I've only known some of you these past two weeks. And I've known some of you since I was a child." She looked at Alisdair. "But one thing I know for certain, is you are my people. My clan. I will stand by my husband's decision to take down Lord Cotswold in this way and I of anyone have more reason to seek revenge against that man. You've known families of other clans who have had their pride wounded and broken at the hands of him, but I have known my own self-pride and body to be broken by him. And I say it is enough. If you strike against the crown of England, it will not be to avenge anyone but your own honor. Show Weatherby that Cotswold's actions have dishonored the very crown he hides behind. Show Weatherby, that although Cotswold may have broken my body, he has never broken my spirit, or that of the clan Claran!"

At her words, the great hall erupted in a wave of cheers, shouts and cry to arms. She knew she had won them over. She and Colin had never spoken truer words to the clan en mass. She knew the hearts of men were roused by the unification and certainty of the leaders they placed their love and loyalty in. She and Colin had never shown them a unified front until now, and they proved every bit as loyal to them and their word, as they had always professed to be.

Audrina held up her dirk and Colin his sword, as the castle halls shook with the loudest cheer yet.

Colin kissed her long and hard in front of everyone as the whoops and whistles and battle cries sounded from his men.

When he broke off the kiss, they turned to the

door together, and hand in hand they marched out into the courtyard. As the Scotsmen swarmed the courtyard, firing flaming arrows into the pyre and the cross, lighting it on fire, at first the English took a step back as the thunderous sound of the marching Scotsman sounded as they emerged, undaunted and unfearful from the castle walls.

Audrina watched from the top of the steps as the pyre burned and the Englishmen scattered from their formations, confused. It wasn't until Cotswold rode through the masses and called them back into formation, that they began to fall in line and surround the clansmen.

Hooded black figures race along the walls of the castle, as the gates were drawn open once more, and the Scotsmen in turn took up position against the English.

It is times like these, Audrina thought, *that truly define a person's character.* She had been given the opportunity to run and hide with the rest of the women and children. But she was not ever that kind of person. She was a fighter. She knew that much as she stared into the outraged face of Lord Cotswold. She knew it the moment she met the haze of red blur from her nightmares about what Cotswold had done to her in that tower. She even knew it when she had faced the thief and chased him down in the museum. She, Audrina, Maeve, MacClaran was never going to run in the face of a fight. She was going to stand her ground and hold fast to what she believed in and she believed in seeking justice against a man who was a monster the likes of Cotswold.

Audrina felt Colin's fingers slip into her own as she felt the rush of power from her love. She had been so loved by her mother and her grandfather. She had been loved by her sisters Catriona and Moira and even by Colin's family. Mary, Donal, Alisdair and even Uncle Dougal had and did love her. The strongest love she felt though, was Colin's love as it warmed her through. She knew that no matter what happened, that love would always win out.

CHAPTER 32

"Witch! Witch!" Cotswold shrieked. He pointed at her as his men formed ranks again. "You've cast your spell on all of them, haven't you! I knew this day would come when the devil himself infiltrated the enemy of England and it has come at last! Witch!" he continued to curse at her.

Colin and she walked slowly toward him. His horse was dancing, threatening to toss him at a moment's notice if the wrong move was made. She understood why the horse was skittish. This much raucous noise and chaos would spook most animals. But she also noted how Cotswold had chosen the horse based on appearance alone. It was a fine-looking animal to be sure, but she guessed that it had never been properly battle trained, if necessary, that was a grave mistake she would prey upon if she needed to.

She did notice that Lord Weatherby's horse stood calmly amongst the fray and din. Lord Weatherby himself, however, barely held a mask of calmness over his visage.

He gritted out, "What manner is this that you destroy the bed on which she will rest if she is proven guilty? This is an affront to the honor of the English code of ethics. It is the most humane way to dispose of a witch if she is so tried and judged to be such a woman possessed of the devil's spirit."

"The only call tae question o'honor here, is Lord Cotswold's honor," Colin called back.

Lord Weatherby raised his eyebrows and sniffed through his enormous nose. "I say, how do you dare speak such a thing? There is an etiquette to be observed here, Lord MacClaran," he thundered.

"Aye, I agree," Colin said. "But ye didnae offer me the same regard when ye stormed the gate and accused me wife o'witchcraft. She should ha'e been given fair trial and a chance tae speak her peace, but Lord Cotswold, shut her down," he responded evenly.

Lord Weatherby seemed to take this into consideration.

But Lord Cotswold rode up, still purple faced with rage. "I told you, no testimony was necessary. My word is law here and it is my word we will be standing on! You have no authority here!" he shouted.

"Actually, my Lord Cotswold," it was Lord Weatherby who interjected on their behalf.

Audrina and Colin remained silent, allowing this to hopefully play out in their favor.

"He does have the authority to demand consideration. When the crown bestowed upon us, the royal duty of partnering with our Scottish brethren, it was with the knowledge, that we would take into consideration, a reasonable request for audience."

"Do you call their aggressive behavior thus far, a reasonable request!" Lord Cotswold shouted at his friend.

"The simplest answer I can give to that is, yes," he replied. "Lord MacClaran has never given the crown cause for concern. I find it hard to believe he would greet fellow Lords in such open hostility without just cause to do so. I for one, would like to hear his reasoning. It would be far simpler for the Claran clan to hand over the witch, and maintain a peaceable relation with the crown, they must have a rousing reason to so vehemently protest the forego of her trial and stand upon your word alone. I will hear that reasoning now," he finished.

Whatever Lord Cotswold was about to retort, was silenced by Lord Weatherby's wave of his hand. Lord Weatherby clearly held a more powerful sway than the two men, because Lord Cotswold blew out a frustrated breath.

"Very well, if you insist on listening to this mad drivel, then let's hear it. Let's hear the reasons they have crafted under the influence of the witch's spell that they would so willingly lay down their lives for her. Do tell us, Lord MacClaran, what is it you wish to say on her behalf?"

Colin smiled at Lord Cotswold, which seemed to unnerve the man. His sneer faltered on his face as he looked back and forth between Lord Weatherby and Colin.

"Actually, t'will be you who has somat tae say on her behalf," he began.

Lord Weatherby leaned forward in his saddle, clearly intrigued by whatever Colin was about to say.

Colin continued, "I ha'e but a few questions. How can ye claim she is a witch, when ye yerself told all and sunder that Maeve here, wandered off when ye were done claimin' yer rights o'Prima Noctem? If she died, why did ye cover tha' up? I ask this, because t'would only make sense if ye were the responsible party," Colin finished.

Apart from the crackling of the fire, not a sound could be heard through the courtyard.

Cotswold's face went white as he looked between Colin and Maeve. It took him a long moment before he began to speak.

"Are you accusing a Lord of the crown of speaking falsehoods? Are you actually going to stand there, in my presence, and profess that I, a Lord and your superior, would commit murder?" he thundered.

Audrina saw his face turn an ugly shade of puce. He could only be feeling the nausea of being confronted by his deeds and accused of lying. He could of course lie some more.

Which was exactly what he tried to do when Lord Weatherby turned to his friend and asked, "What's this he speaks of? What is the truth in this? Does he speak true words to me? Upon your honor and that of the crown, speak up man!"

"I...I...I did let the witch go. It was after she

had wandered off that I learnt she was murdered!" he stammered.

His fear grew evident upon his face as Weatherby stared between them all. He had obviously been blind to his friend's habits, and he may have heard rumors, but he had brushed them aside in favor of the honor he believed the Lords of the English crown held. Weatherby was a shrewd man and knew of the open hostilities between the Scots and the English. He was well aware that rumors abounded because of these hostilities. He himself had worked tirelessly and diligently to be a fair ruler, and not be prey to their devastating effects.

"Tell me, man, you were supposed to return the bride to her home via a safe journey and escort. You just let her wander off to be murdered? And then you did nothing to assuage the rumors that surrounded you? Why didn't you see to your duties to remain honorable? Her clan, if it is to be believed, should have been given recompense for her plight. What is the meaning of these atrocities?" Lord Weatherby's calm resolve was cracking under the pressure of his immense distaste for Lords who abused their power.

Lord Cotswold could only stammer in terror as the man rounded on him.

Audrina took this as her opportunity to pounce on the weakened Lord Cotswold's resolve. She looked up at Colin, finding support in his eyes as she stepped forward to confront her tormentor, torturer, and murderer.

CHAPTER 33

A
udrina took a deep breath and stepped forward. Lord Weatherby looked at her in a new light. It was no longer with passive indifference, but he clearly wanted her side of the story, if only to add to the story in an attempt to clarify things.

"Lord Cotswold, how can you claim that I was killed and raised from the dead by black magic if you had no idea what happened to me? Which is it? Did you or didn't you know what happened? What about all the other missing brides from neighboring clans? Do you know what happened to them? You have made claims that they all wandered off too, but then you have spoken of their murders. Please, tell us all, what is the truth of it?" Audrina said her peace and all of the bluster blew out of her. She wanted this ordeal to be over with. She wanted to be upstairs, in her bed with Colin, making love and falling asleep in his arms when they were done.

A bone-weary tiredness came over her. She was so raw and emotional at the mistreatment of Lord Cotswold, and she simply didn't understand how a man as vile as he, could have gotten away with hurting so many people. What justice was there in the order of things if men like him were allowed to roam free? How could the Scots ever rally themselves to the cause in the face of such adversity? She had seen the movie Braveheart. She had recognized the romanticized version that had been spun. But this was reality. It was hard and cold and cruel and men like Cotswold often won because of their power and money, and it just wasn't fair. If he didn't break now, there was no telling what he would get away with. In an instant, Audrina felt the scots people who had to face the harsh reality of the unfairness of the English rule. It wasn't like in romance novels, her favored genre. The good guys didn't always win, and there was a huge chance, it could all go wrong for them tonight if Cotswold somehow weaseled his way out of this.

Audrina wanted to believe in the unending hope of the Scots will for a severed tie from England and the right to rule and govern their own people. But she knew the fate of Scotland and what they had to endure through the centuries. She knew that they may have won their freedom briefly in a few years, but the war would wage on for centuries, resulting in the same fateful outcome of the Jacobite uprising. Audrina found herself sinking in a sea of emotions and despair. How did the people always manage to pull themselves up during their time of greatest need, and hold on to an ideal that somehow saw them through the worst of it all, so that they remained a people and civilization that survived to the modern world, rich with history and culture and love?

In an instant, Audrina knew that was the answer. Love was the answer. The Scottish people had a love for kin and country that was undefined by any other nation. It went deeper somehow than just the blood of their relatives. They found love through the magic in the country itself. Audrina knew it wasn't just her love with Colin that had brought her back. The sun shone down on Scotland in a light that was unlike any other country across the world. There was something special here, a special magic. Audrina lifted her spirits and her unnerving fatigue as she looked at Colin. He was the epitome of that love and magic, and she took strength in him as he gazed back at her. She found the threads of her courage in the knowledge that, even if they didn't win this night, somehow, Scotland would bring her back to her Highlander.

Audrina was tired, but she was alert enough to recognize the instant his resolve cracked. Lord Weatherby was about to question him further, clearly having no knowledge of other missing and deceased brides when Lord Cotswold began to laugh. It was a sickening laugh as he inwardly revealed in the memories of his victims. He'd finally been found out. There was no denying it now. Lord Weatherby backed away from him as he opened his mouth and began screaming at her in a psychotic rage. Soldiers crowded around both English and Scottish alike as Cotswold raged. Some protected their Lord Weatherby, some protected Cotswold from bringing harm to himself as he stormed around and hollered at her.

"How the bloody hell can you be standing there, you little bitch! I strangled you with my bare hands when you head butted me while I had you pinned down. I took you like the pig you are and then let my men have their way with your broken body. I thought all the fight had left you as I went back for another round, but then you surprised me, you threw your head back and smashed into my teeth, causing me to lose one." He pointed to his missing and chipped tooth.

Lord Weatherby looked on in horror at his friend's confession. Lord Cotswold ignored him, only having eyes for the woman who was the victim who refused to cower before him and had finally driven him mad. He could not understand how she had bested him. He didn't know her secret and he desperately needed to know. He was the master of deception and gleaner of knowledge. He sadistically enjoyed ripping everything he could from a person and watched them drown in a pool of their own horror as they realized he had stripped away the vestiges of their pride and dignity. He had spies everywhere and he knew everything, and yet this woman had bested him finally at his own game. The knowledge was what drove him mad. The knowledge that she held something from him, a Lord entitled, and he couldn't figure out how to take it from her. He screamed in frustration as he occasionally lunged for her. She stood her ground, unwavering and unflinching in his rage. Colin remained at her side as he confessed all, there to offer aid if Lord Cotswold attempted one last try for her life.

"When you broke my teeth, I wrapped my hands around your pretty neck and squeezed until the life drained out of you while I took you. When I was done with you, I had you thrown to the pig slops! It's no secret hogs will eat anything. Even dead flesh. I came back two days later, content that they had torn you to pieces and left you reduced to nothing but the excrement they rolled around in, in their pig sty! How did you raise yourself from the dead? It must have been a pact with the devil himself, if not by some black magic? You weren't the first. I used and discarded all the brides I was forced to perform my duties upon. They met the same fate you did amongst my pigs. There were thirteen of you altogether. Thirteen years I have been forced to live in these vermin infested waste-lands amongst the Scots. So, I took thirteen of them for every year I had to waste amongst them. And every year the Christmas hog that was slaughtered was fattened on the slop of your bodies. But you, how did you rise from the dead? I gorged myself last Christmas on that hog to the point of being sick. How did you do it!" he shrieked at her.

CHAPTER 34

Audrina felt sick. She had never known what had happened to Maeve's body. No one had. Everyone had assumed Cotswold had them buried or thrown to the scavengers in the wild, never to be seen from again. No one suspected that he himself was the evidentiary proof of where they had ended up, as was testament to his bulging girth at his belt.

Audrina wasn't the only one who felt bile rise in the back of her throat. Lord Cotswold's words rang through the courtyard in a sickening, self-sabotaging barrage of words that he had spit forward. If anyone was called into question about the events that night, they wouldn't be able to lie. There were too many witnesses to his proclamation. Too many people knew of the disgusting treachery, and the vile depths of his depravity. Audrina heard the distinctive sounds of retching coming from behind her and even from a few of the other English higher ranks. Clearly, they had partaken in Cotswold's Christmas feasts too. It took a long moment before anyone sprang into action. Audrina noticed the slightest of gestures from Lord Weatherby as he commanded a few men forward.

A few of Lord Weatherby's men stepped forward and hauled him down from his horse. Lord Weatherby himself looked pale and held a handkerchief to his mouth, breathing slowly. He gazed upon his former friend with the look of condemnation of a madman. Lord Cotswold continued to scream at her, demanding she tell him how she had risen from the dead.

Confusion seemed to ensue as people, realizing his confession, not hers, was the end of the standoff. The men who had been hiding in the chapel, but had heard everything, emerged behind the English ranks which caused them to raise their swords in alarm. The men high up on the walls scaled the ladders and came down for a better look at the raving English mad man, and the wee woman who bested him with naught but a slight of her hand and words.

Colin continued to retain control of his men, signaling to them that they should not attack unless attacked, and the men all looked warily from Cotswold, to Colin, to Audrina, to Lord Weatherby. A light murmur began to ripple through the crowd as they reiterated Lord Cotswold's words.

Audrina heard whispers of, "cannibal," "barbaric" and of course, "mad man."

She felt a wave of relief as the realization that it was over began to sink in. As the men were still gathered around, there was still that small chance of a skirmish, but the louder the buzz became of Lord Cotswold's downfall and disgrace, the more the reality sank in. She contemplated turning on her heel and walking back into the castle, never to set her eyes on Lord Cotswold again. She was remiss that she had never looked into what his fate had been when she had the information and internet readily available at her fingertips. She realized, it didn't matter now though. She may not understand medieval law and justice, but judging by the look on Lord Weatherby's face, there would at least be some small measure of assurance that Lord Cotswold would be dealt with.

Audrina looked at Cotswold who was pale faced and sweating. She wondered how she had ever feared such a man. She was grateful that even though she knew the fate of Maeve's body, she never had to truly endure the nightmares of how her body ended up being in that pig sty. She had feared the red haze that had appeared over her vision when Cotswold burst through the door of the tower, now she was grateful for it as it offered some small amount of discretion from the true horrors of what Cotswold had been capable of. Audrina decided right then and there, if there was ever a time to enact her revenge, if she ever needed the resolution to the man who had been the bane of her existence but to Maeve's, Colin's and countless other souls as well, now was the time. She fortified herself and her emotions before she approached. She knew exactly what she needed to say to seek her revenge. She knew exactly the kind of effect it would have on a man like Cotswold. Strangely, it gave her no self-satisfying purpose, save for the fact that she knew it was being said in the name and honor of Maeve and all that had been done to her.

Audrina stepped forward as Lord Cotswold heaved against the restraint of his guards. Colin tried to stop her, but she turned to him and cupped his cheek. Tears streamed down his handsome face. He had never known what had happened to his wife and knowing was perhaps now worse than had he never found out.

"It will be alright," she said calmly. "He can't hurt us now." Audrina gave him a reassuring look and wiped his tears away. She wanted to tell him that Maeve was at peace. She knew it because she shared her soul, but she simply didn't have the words yet to comfort a man who had been grieving the loss of what was right in front of him, for over a year now. Audrina let the tears coat her fingers, and she discovered as she made another vow to herself, that she was the kind of woman who was true to her word and honor, and that was a testament as any, to her noble Scottish blood. She vowed she would endeavor to never be the cause of Colin's tears again, save for tears of happiness. She knew he would suffer loss and sadness, that was a part of life, but she was never going to be the weapon forged in a mold of flesh that was used against him in such cruel ways again.

She kissed his cheek and tasted his tears on her lips. She licked the salt away, realizing the power of Scotia lay in the emotions of her people. The land was forged of blood, sweat and tears, and in turn bore sons and daughters who felt as proudly as the

Scots did. She smiled at him and turned back to her quarry.

Colin let go of her arm and she stepped up to Lord Cotswold. She lowered her voice, so he strained his ears to her. He stunk of sweat and unwashed flesh. Audrina felt her gag reflexes kick in, and she wondered at how she had endured the night with him. She almost felt relief that Maeve had found solace in her death, as she was then not forced to endure the disgusting feel of that man using her in such vile ways.

Audrina took a deep breath and whispered to him. She held her breath as he realized the meaning of her words. Without condemning herself, she revealed the truth to him.

"You want to know why it was me? Why I was the one to escape your clutches whether in this life or another? Unlucky thirteen remember? I was the thirteenth." She blew out her breath as she stepped back.

Her revenge was found as his face went from confused to fearful to anger once more. He began screaming at her again, nonsensical babble as Lord Weatherby ushered to his men to drag him away.

Lord Weatherby turned to his men and Lord Cotswold's to issue a command to leave. The men began to lower their swords and turned, marching out the gates, unwavering or questioning Lord Weatherby's authority.

Lord Weatherby turned back to Colin and Audrina with a sad look on his face. He had never suspected the depths of which his friend had sunk.

"I will call upon you, Lord MacClaran, to reset the bonds of unity and civility once Lord Cotswold is tried in London for his activities. With any luck, he will be seen by the finest healers London has to offer and taken in by the care of his family. I will claim the acting capacity of his position, until such a time that the crown sees fit to usher in someone in my stead. I do not know what has transpired here, beyond the mental breaking of a man I once held in high regard, let us pray for his speedy recovery."

With that, Lord Weatherby turned his horse and followed his party out the gate.

CHAPTER 35

S ix months later Audrina lay in bed next to Colin, playing a game of chess. She knew it to be different in the modern societies, but the game had been around since the sixth century, and Colin had proved to be a worthy opponent, as he was very adept at the game.

Audrina moved her queen along the board, having grown better at strategizing in the last few months as fall had set upon them, and winter's harsh omens began to arise. Early morning frosts could be seen on the decaying grasses of the fen. Bessie's breath froze on the air whenever she blew her snout at Audrina. But Audrina was content with her life in Castle Claran.

She had many months now to reflect on that night when they had finally caused the downfall of

Lord Cotswold. He had been replaced by one of his kin, who was a younger and more adept Lord at adapting to the harsh way of life in Scotland. He had proved thus far to be far more sound of mind and reasonable than his predecessor.

Colin had let Audrina be privy to that conversation when the young, nervous Lord rode in with a small group of soldiers. After the last invasion, he was not greeted so warmly as the Claran's notable hospitality was renowned for. Lord Bryce was a young Lord, acting under the instruction of Lord Weatherby and he had been charged with this region as a test to determine his capabilities of Lordship. His mentor, Lord Weatherby had stayed true to his word and largely left them in peace, opting to send a courier once a month to convey messaged and declarations of the crown. With hostilities arising from the other clans, he had been weary of making further enemies of the Claran clan.

Audrina reflected on the day when Lord Bryce walked into the great hall. He had been announced, but she had almost felt sorry for him as the men unsheathed their dirks and toyed with the blades, cleaning out under their fingernails in a veiled threat. The young lord had twirled his riding cap in his hands, his fidgeting a sure sign of his greenery in his vocation. He had spoken clearly, but with a note of apprehension as he looked around at the men, and his own men twitched nervously under the watchful eye of the Scotsmen.

"I have come to sustain the relationship that has been built between you and Lord Weatherby, upon his command. I would offer my hand in friendship and civility, to let it be known that this allegiance between the Scottish clans and the Crown, be continued further. I would also like to make mention, that upon the mentorship of Lord Weatherby, I am but his humble and honorable apprentice, and that I seek no personal gain from this allegiance, nor do I make any claim to uphold the rights of Prima Noctem. Hence forth, Lord Weatherby has disbanded the right from any of his charges he Lords over, and I am happily and newly married." Lord Bryce's voice quavered from time to time, but he made it through his rehearsed speech.

Audrina was cautious, but felt for him. He didn't look a day older than eighteen or nineteen, which would put him at a younger age than they were. He was fairly green all around in his marriage and his duties, and she saw the look of acknowledgement when Colin understood this too. He would have the upper hand here, but being an honorable man himself, he wouldn't abuse the young Lord.

"What has become o'Lord Cotswold?" Colin demanded. He needed to assert his authority now, and there would be plenty of time later to test the bonds of the arrangements honor.

"Let it be known that mine uncle, Lord Cotswold, has been returned unto the folds of the family in disgrace. The crown has seen fit to grant mercy, in that his mind is not of a sound nature, but he has been stripped of his titles and lands, and they have been dispensed to more suitable and able Lords." He looked at Audrina in terror then. As if he was waiting for her to find something unreasonable in this.

She remembered Lord Weatherby's words about praying for Lord Cotswold's recovery. She personally hoped he fell in a pig sty himself and met the same fate as his victim's, but it would serve no purpose but to assuage her own insidious need for revenge. She had taken enough the night he was taken away. Colin had grilled her as to what she had said to him that night, but she kissed him and told him it was not anything to concern himself over.

Audrina knew the number thirteen was unlucky. She knew the number was often associated with bad luck, misfortune, and ill wishes. In many cultures across many religions and time periods, it was associated with witches. She was certain Lord Cotswold had picked up her meaning when she had told him she had been his unlucky thirteen. His face had paled as he realized she answered his continued question about how she had done it. How she had risen from the dead. Without actually saying so, she had told him that she had done it via witchcraft. His suspicions and accusations had been right all along, but no one believed him because he had just cast himself into the subjugating light of a mad man.

Audrina smiled serenely at Lord Bryce as he looked at her. If anyone was to believe Lord Cotswold's proclamations now, it would be his own family. Audrina had a suspicion that he may have forewarned Lord Bryce, but Lord Bryce was shrewd enough not to express his suspicions. Or his was just plain scared to and truly believed she would curse him.

In any event, Lord Bryce left that day without suffering at the hands of the men his uncle had tormented for so long. Audrina didn't think they would be seeing him often, and she was fine with that.

As she moved her king into place, Audrina continued to reflect on the last six months. She had settled into life at Claran Castle with relative ease. The people had accepted her without question after that night. She heard tales whispered through the streets of her bravery and courage at standing up to Lord Cotswold and they whispered of her magic, not of a black magic, but that she was blessed with the gift from Scotia's own magics. She had settled into a way of life, healing the people who came to her and finding the trust they placed in their new lady of the castle to be touching. Donal would often follow her around, swearing to protect her against any more harm from the Sassenach soldiers. He idolized her as much as he did Colin.

Even Alisdair found a sense of peace and began courting Aine, the blacksmith's daughter. It turned out the blacksmith was their cousin and Aine had been given a place in the castle to work. There was no longer the fear of Prima Noctem held over their marriage beds, and Audrina suspected a spring time wedding was to be had. Mary had gratefully retired her position as Lady of the house and was content to work on crafting the tapestries that Audrina had discovered she was the artist of. They soothed her and despite the fine weaving and needle work, helped her to relax and relieve her tension headaches.

Donal had decided it was time to not shirk his responsibilities, but instead endeavored to learn how to become a man and no longer gave his mother a run for her money. Instead he occasionally jested with Audrina and told her she was a fierce Scottish warrior in another life, the way she had stood up to Cotswold like that. Audrina was also pleased to discover the ornery behavior of her beloved pet Bessie, was due in part to the fact that the "mad old coo" as Alisdair had dubbed her, was due at some point in the spring. From what Colin told her, it was expected that she was carrying twins, which delighted Audrina to no end, because like Maeve, she could be found in the stables singing to her pet and her unborn calves and it was often the lullaby she learned from her grandfather.

Colin had continued to woo her and show his devotion and love on a daily basis, and he brought her books so that she could read. She didn't mind that they were religious. She found she had a new peace and faith with religion and God. She was finally content with the knowledge that Maeve rested and she carried on. She had gotten used to being called Maeve. It didn't upset her to answer to it when someone called out to her. She felt honored to carry the mantle.

He had also taken her to Skye that fall. Before the harshness of winter made the trails impassable and at a time when the spray of the sea on the island kissed the golden cliffs and sparkled along the brilliant foliage. She had found a simpler way of life there than even the castle. She hadn't thought it was possible. She occasionally missed modern amenities, but it wasn't anything she couldn't cope without.

She had found the gravestones of her sisters in Skye. They had a Gaelic blessing etched on them which Colin had translated for her. She was even learning to speak a few words herself. It was there that she laid Maeve to rest. Colin watched as she dug a small hole next to her sister's graves and buried the kilt pin. She had no doubt it had served its purpose in returning her to her love. Her love and Colin's had spanned not only distance, but centuries of time as well until it had brought them back together.

Audrina ran her fingers over the blessing etched in the stone, and realized it wasn't just a spell, but an epitaph for her sisters as well.

"Bone of my bone, flesh of my flesh, through spans of time, I cannot rest. Seek thee my kin, and pardon my sin, that I may reincarnate, and new life begin. And with this pin I shall be returned to my love, cast through the ages, by touch of mine blood, and light from sun up above."

AUDRINA CLUTCHED HER STOMACH AS SHE TRACED the small print. Colin had yet to catch on to the small gesture, she was waiting for the right moment to tell him. She stood and swayed on her feet, Colin assuming it was because she was tired from the journey.

"No," she proclaimed. "It is probably that the two little ones that have been growing in me for the last two months I have missed my flux, tap the energy from me," she finally confessed.

Colin stared at her in shock. "How do ye ken it, lass?" he whispered as his hand went to her belly.

"There's just some things a woman knows," she told him.

He bent down on one knee and placed his head on her belly. They were high on a cliff overlooking the sea, but they were the only ones around.

Colin looked up at her with passion in his eyes. "I cannae believe it, lass!" he whispered in excitement.

"I know, neither can I," she said. But she found she was happy with the knowledge. "Colin, will you do me a favor and consider the name Dougal Argus MacClaran for the boy, and for his sister, Catriona Moira MacClaran?" she asked breathlessly. She did not know how to explain to him how she knew. It appeared as if her sisters had blessed her with one last gift of their blood vow. As she had touched the words etched in the stone, she had been gifted the premonition of the babies she was carrying in her belly. Apparently, the love of family was carried through time, and she was to find Colin's Uncle Dougal, her grandfather and her sisters reincarnated within the souls of her unborn children.

"Aye, tis a lovely set o'names for the wee bairns," he said kissing her stomach again.

She and Colin hastily made their way back down to the encampment they were sleeping in for the night, and there she had shown Colin she was good on her vow to prove to him she would show her love daily with kisses.

When she took him in her mouth, he gasped and rose up off the bed, trying to draw her up the length of his body. She placed a firm hand on the flat of his belly and pushed him back down as she administered her kisses. She felt powerful as she looked up at the highlander writhing in ecstasy for her under her administrations. Colin had cried out to her, begging to be allowed to claim her and she denied him several times as he had teased Maeve before their wedding. His resolve had finally broke and he pushed his way up, flipping her gently onto her back and claiming her as he swiftly dipped in between her legs. Later that night he had shown her the beauty of torture of a different nature as he returned the same kisses to her.

When they had returned to Castle Claran, the re-opened the chapel and celebrated with the whole clan in a wedding celebration that had been denied them. Audrina was insistent that their babies be Christened in the chapel, and as Colin had a renewed faith himself and he proclaimed the children in her belly to be his miracles, he readily agreed to her request, allowing the new priest to reside within the chapel.

Audrina lay on the bed palming the queen in her hand before she made a move.

"What are ye thinkin' o', lass, in tha' head o' yers?" Colin asked.

"I was just reminiscing about the last six months," she confessed.

"Aye? What in particular?" he asked.

She cast a glance sideways at his rough parchment where he had begun to sketch a drawing of her and her swollen belly.

"A little bit of everything," she told him. "I was thinking of the night when we finally won, and I was thinking of everything that has happened since."

"Aye, ye ne'er did tell me what ye said tae him, my Highland Queen." He gathered her in his arms as she placed the queen back on the board in the position she wanted it in.

"Aye told him what every queen does when she wins, checkmate."

ABOUT REBECCA PRESTON

Rebecca lives in New York City with her dog. She loves sweet love stories with great characters. She loves traveling the world and experiencing new cities and cultures. Jane Austen is her favorite author.

Sign up below!
eepurl.com/c-chk9

ALSO BY REBECCA PRESTON

Jane Austen Fan Fiction

Arranged To Darcy
A Convenient Darcy Marriage
Married To Darcy

Printed in Great Britain
by Amazon

61321996R00203